I0831749

The Second Baptism of Albert Simmel

The Second Baptism of Albert Simmel

A Novel

Rodney Clapp

CASCADE *Books* • Eugene, Oregon

THE SECOND BAPTISM OF ALBERT SIMMEL
A Novel

Cascade Books
An Imprint of Wipf and Stock Publishers
199 W. 8th Ave., Suite 3
Eugene, OR 97401

www.wipfandstock.com

PAPERBACK ISBN: 978-1-61097-107-2
HARDCOVER ISBN: 978-1-4982-8532-2
EBOOK ISBN: 978-1-4982-9986-2

Cataloguing-in-Publication data:

Names: Last, First. | other names in same manner

Title: The second baptism of Albert Simmel : a novel / Rodney Clapp.

Description: Eugene, OR: Cascade Books, 2016 | Includes bibliographical references and index.

Identifiers: ISBN 978-1-61097-107-2 (paperback) | ISBN 978-1-4982-8532-2 (hardcover) | ISBN 978-1-4982-9986-2 (ebook)

Subjects: LCSH: Fiction. | Title.

Classification: PS3623.I578 S35 2016 (print) | PS3623.I578 (ebook)

Manufactured in the U.S.A.

To my brother, Kerry, and my sister, Kimberly, who first learned storytelling—as did I—at our grandparents' wonderful dinner tables.

1

Decades ago, when the people called Americans still thought of their country as young and its promises inexhaustible, these surroundings were all different. Albert ruminated on this in the dusk, ending one more long workday with the trudge home from the train station. He walked in what formerly was called a suburb. But he did not walk on a sidewalk. He stepped freely, casually, down the middle westbound lane of a six-lane freeway of Old Chicago.

Other pedestrians streamed along the same roadway. The vast stretch of lanes, seventy or eighty feet across, had been built to accommodate speeding automobiles and behemoth tractor-trailers. The freeway was the size of a substantial river, and once it had clogged and roared with traffic, a whitewater estuary frothing on a concrete and asphalt bed. Now there was no traffic other than foot traffic. A few pedestrians walked in pairs, talking quietly. But most sojourned apart, several arms' lengths from the closest walker. Far from white water gorged and rushing, the freeway was tonight, as on every night for a long while, a mostly dry riverbed. Here and there trickled the currents of pedestrians. And soon, with the sunset, these intermittent currents would cease.

As Albert knew from his mother, and from books, the suburbs were once inhabited by the relatively wealthy, the so-called "middle class." These days there was no middle class. The decidedly wealthy lived in the core city, at the east end of the commuter train line Al had just ridden. Mother said the suburbs had been referred to fondly as the "'burbs," a term that made Albert think of "burps" or "blurbs," things comfortable and innocuous and mildly amusing. Babies burped, and books were reassuringly blurbed by the author's friends. For as long as Albert himself could remember, however, people called the suburbs the "subs." This emphasized that they were the home of the underclass, the subordinate folk who subsisted on vegetables and eggs collected from backyard coops, who toiled for the rich city-dwellers or cobbled together a series of handyman and odd jobs. Or just went without work and resorted to other means of survival.

The surface Al and others trod on was no longer smooth and unbroken. Even in their heyday, the freeways incorrigibly cracked and potholed. Lacking constant maintenance, the roads' cracks widened, their potholes yawned open into what Al supposed would better be designated kettle-holes or cauldron-holes. After heavy rains, the holes filled and a duck or two might float on the larger ones. Weeds and wildflowers heaved up through the cracks in the pavement. Not only weeds and wildflowers: trees, saplings and medium-sized pines and oaks and elms, stood at intervals. In especially overgrown stretches, blanched white cement split into jagged squares and rectangles, resembling tombstones lying flat and scattered in a bombed cemetery. All this made the freeways passable only for foot transit and the infrequent bicyclist or horseback rider.

Albert arrived at a corridor where the freeway was adjoined on both sides by the ruins of shopping malls. The hastily constructed, gargantuan boxed buildings had at many places collapsed. At others walls and sagging semblances of roofs remained, though no plate glass windows were still whole. Strangely, what best endured were flimsy plastic signs. In garish if now faded colors, they skewed atop the rubble piles of walls that had long ago crumbled, roosted on rusty poles now bent and leaning. The ruins loomed at a considerable distance from the road. They were surrounded by vast, flat, ruptured parking lots. Albert imagined that the parking lots had once been like encircling deserts, where shoppers abandoned their vehicles and hiked toward the stores as if they were oases.

What surprised Albert was not that the malls were currently unsightly and uninviting. He lived in a world full of the decaying structures of another era. He was struck more by the fact that those who built and eagerly frequented the shopping emporia apparently really did regard them almost as paradises, as oases. And this to an extent that they never noticed that the buildings and parking lots were unattractive, that they were not visually pleasing destinations at which to arrive or among which to wander and pass time. Historians Al had read emphasized that in the period at the height of the malls' popularity, great emphasis was laid on the functionality of architecture. Stores were built simply to contain (some were even called "big box stores") and to shelter, as briefly as possible, the goods that visitors would rush to buy and remove to their own premises. Customers, it seemed, were so fixed and concentrated on the function of shopping that they lost awareness of the environment in which they spent entire days of their lives. No wonder the heedless, mindlessly acquisitive inhabitants of this earlier era were known in Al's day as "squandrels."

But now Al realized he was dallying. The evening shadows lengthened at his back. The sun was falling faster, the sky leaching its blue and turning red. Unlike the forebears who had ambled obliviously amid the malls, at various hours of the day or night, Albert could not afford to lose attention to his surroundings, or linger here after dark. He resumed a more deliberate pace. Ahead he saw lanes that split off from the freeway. They would curve, then loop, on to a smaller road that plunged between older, taller trees, into a neighborhood of houses with sprawling backyards, partly inhabited apartment complexes, taverns, shops, and churches. There, before darkness gathered into an impenetrable mass unpunctuated by electric lighting, Albert Simmel would be home.

Albert pulled to and locked the heavy wooden door. Typically he climbed the outside stairs and entered directly into his flat, the rehabbed top floor of the Episcopal Church of St. Brendan the Wanderer. But tonight he wasn't hungry. He left the open air through the church's front door. Something—he thought it was the doe and her fawn intent on berries blocks from his home, near enough to an Edenic belt of woods to remain relaxed, and gracefully craning their necks and peering at him out of shining obsidian eyes—something put him in a mood of loss. Al probed with a hand and rested a palm against the cool stone wall, waiting for his eyesight to adjust. Soon the blindness left him and the dim evening light bloomed through colored glass. Speckled in filtered greens and purples, he made his way across the narthex to the rear of the sanctuary. He lighted four candles: one for a church friend who recently succumbed to influenza, one for Granddad Madison, one for his father. And one for Valerie, sweet Valerie. He sat in a wickered chair near the candles. He pictured and prayed for each loved one, but it was Valerie, far and away it was Valerie, he missed more than any other. He missed her so much his ribs ached. He missed her so much his teeth hurt.

Of his grandparents, Granddad Madison, gone now for a dozen years, had affected Al the most. He was a short, barrel-chested man with eyeglasses and one bright streak of silver at the front of his thick hair. He worked twelve hours a day at the drugstore he and Grandma operated, and still had energy to burn. A few years after he and Grandma bought a home, Granddad decided they needed a basement. He hand-dug it right under the standing house. Over time he experimented with a series of hobbies, from woodworking to toy train tableaux to guitar playing. He nurtured a flower garden and grew miniature cacti traveling salesmen delivered at the store. And every night from dark to one or two in the morning, he read.

Among Albert's favorite childhood memories were overnights at Grandma and Granddad Madison's house. After Grandma had gone to bed, Granddad and Albert rested in two leather chairs, reading their respective books. Albert occupied Grandma's special chair, but only after she had evacuated it for the day. (No one except Granddad ever sat in his chair, even if Granddad wasn't anywhere near the house.) Al and Granddad Madison drank bottled soda and munched on salty peanuts. At intervals Granddad asked where Al was in some story Granddad had recommended and plucked from his shelves. When Al provided details, Granddad smiled and gazed out the blank night window, as if he were recalling some lost friend or distant golden event of his youth. Then, often, the old man would exclaim, "Oh, I want to read that again!" Dropping his current book into his lap like a neglected pet, he took Albert's book, flexed the spine and pressed his fingers down the gutter with delectation, leaned forward, and began reading aloud. He read intensely if not boomingly (Grandma was asleep in the next room), speeding his pace as the plot surged, slowing with savor over sumptuous descriptions, chortling in delight as he repeated especially admired lines. During these impromptu readings he occasionally stopped abruptly, even at mid-sentence. He raised a knee, gouged one elbow deep into the armrest of his chair, tipped to one side like a sailboat struck by a sudden gale, and let loose a ripe, long fart. Then, as if he hadn't even paused, he resumed his recitation.

Al remembered Granddad Madison to God. He next shifted attention to his father, buried now for four years. His dad had died in his mid-sixties when he succumbed to a respiratory virus. Ray Simmel had been legendary, at least within the family, for his toughness. He delivered mail, which meant riding horseback fifteen miles a day, four days a week. Albert had heard of a motto from the Old American postal service, about getting the mail through in rain, sleet, or snow. But what his father truly dreaded was lightning. On at least half a dozen occasions bolts had crashed close enough to, as Ray put it, "singe the hair on my balls." He described the preliminary iron odor and taste on his tongue, the prickly sensation across his back and legs. Then within moments a monumental spear of light, wider than a tree trunk and white as ivory in the noon sun, would split the sky and stab into the ground. The strike deafened. It stunned all the senses. Usually Ray had found shelter in an abandoned building or under a freeway overpass, but once a storm closed too rapidly for him to dismount and stake his horse. The lightning strike temporarily blinded the terrified animal, which ran into the side of a house and broke its neck. Ray staggered home, soaked and bruised, and was back on his route two days later.

Given so much that Ray Simmel had survived, it was all the more bitterly ironic that one January he took a cold, and could not shake it. He hacked vile, bilious sputum for weeks, then went feverish and descended into a coma. It was the first time in Albert's entire life that his father was bedridden. With the quarrels over his son's relationship with Valerie, Ray and Al had not been friendly for years. By the time Ray lay unconscious and incommunicative for three days, Al felt the anxiety rise on him like floodwater. He found himself sitting sentinel beside what surely would become a deathbed. He gave his father up as lost to the world, and wished he had spoken affectionate words while Ray could still hear them. Late the next afternoon, he took the hand of the husk that had been his father, squeezed it, and declared, "I love you, Dad." Immediately, firmly, the hand squeezed back. Startled, Al jerked his hand from his father's grip. It was as though he had been grabbed by a ghost, embraced through the veil of mortality. So it was that Albert added one more regret to the long chronicle of his sorrowful war with Ray Simmel: the regret that when his father had tried, one last time, to make peace and heal the breach, Albert had responded as if bitten by a rattlesnake. In hours the elder Simmel really was dead. Two days later he rested in his grave. Recalling the moment after all these years, Al muttered, "Lord, have mercy." *Was that a prayer or a cry in the dark?* he wondered. *Was there a difference?*

He turned his thoughts to Valerie. Her hazel eyes and shoulder-length hair flashed in his mind. That was all he could stand. He rose from the wickered chair and proceeded upstairs.

Situated just off the kitchen of Al's second-story apartment was the spacious living room. Behind it ran a long hallway, leading to three bedrooms. There were bay windows across the front of the living room. The recessed windows looked directly out into the leafy canopies of trees. The elevation, with its tunneling length, made the apartment feel like a cave in the sky. Al burrowed into the rearmost, master bedroom. Before long he slept.

He dreamed. He was at a house in the mountains. A huge wooden deck jutted off one side of the house. Before the deck was an enormous, absolutely still lake. In the odd way of dreams, he somehow knew that lake was as deep as it was beautiful. The place was busy with relatives, bustling with Albert's uncles and aunts and cousins and nephews and nieces. The door of the house giving onto the deck was left wide open. From the door issued a grandmother with a cherry pie on one hand and a pumpkin pie on another. Mother trailed with a thick, fudge-frosted chocolate cake. Children sensed the arrival of desserts and dashed across the lawn toward tables on the deck. Grownups clustered in conversational pods continued their talk and laughter, but followed the food with their eyes.

Then Granddad Madison, who had already been dead for years, appeared at the reunion. He was not frightening. No one was shocked at the ghost, but no one spoke to him or remarked on his company. The comfortable babble of the living, of folk who knew one another at their worst as well as their best and had nothing to hide, carried on uninterrupted. Granddad strolled among the family, assuming the slightly sheepish smile of a man arrived late at an appointment.

And there, there at the edge of the deck, stood Dad. Like Granddad, he too had died. He too was unthreatening. He too was mute. Unable to resist, Albert approached and greeted him. But Dad could not, he did not, speak. Even his eyes did not answer. His absence ached harder, his unbridgeable distance was rendered more keenly real, by this strange presence without presence. He was a cipher, written in body English intact but baffling, legible but defying interpretation.

Then Al heard a voice. It called to him, once, then twice, rising in volume. It sounded like Valerie's voice, the lovely music of Valerie's voice. He turned and there she stood, just out of the water at the edge of the lake. She wore a summer dress with her freckled shoulders naked. She raised a tanned arm and curled her fingers in beckoning. "Albert," she said. "Albert. Come here."

Al started from his sleep. He sat up, gasping. For the first time in this familiar, recurrent dream, the dead had spoken.

2

In successive days Al untangled what it was about the dream that made it so unsettling. It was not that it reminded him of Valerie. He never forgot Valerie. She came to mind on countless occasions daily—in the build and step of a woman who walked ahead of him, in a kitchen or bakery at the smell of fresh bread that she loved so much. The most routine thing could do it. On a bright, cloudless spring day he would think of their affectionate running argument: he said such days were "sunny," while Val insisted they were better thought of as "blue-sky" days. But the more piquant, stabbing memories came with peculiar stimulants, on unpredictable occasions.

Once, for instance, he was drinking in a bar and a crusty guy in a fedora climbed on a small platform with an acoustic guitar. The bottleneck slide did it. The rattle and keening of the strings conjured the full scene. The very first time she heard the country blues, in a bar nearly identical to the one he was in, Valerie had stopped talking and was entranced by the musician. A tear welled up in one eye. Albert was captivated by the music, but at that moment even more by this beautiful woman. He saw the tear swell, then, like a salmon leaping a dam, clear her lower eyelid. It streaked down her cheek and she did not wipe away its track until the song was done.

So thoughts of her—reincarnated feelings of her—were nothing different, even if they were not entirely pleasant. Neither was it new or especially disturbing to meet Valerie in a dream. She had appeared in many dreams, as had his deceased father and grandfather. Yet she (like they) had never spoken. In the dreams and in the waking memories she had seemed a kind of ineffectual or—yes, a *dead* presence—something you coped with and worked around, but never really had to respond to or actively engage, exactly because it had no life or volition of its own.

Albert decided it was like someone who had a bum hand, bereft of movement and any sensation except frequent stabs of pain. You learned how to get along with one hand, you developed tricks and ploys to endure and sometimes avoid the pain. In the company of others possessing two healthy hands, when performing menial chores or making love, you were constantly reminded that you had only one hand, but the reminders were no longer piercing. They had dulled with time and familiarity. They had become, simply, a part of you. But then say that somehow the bad hand appeared to regain its vitality. Suddenly you could feel it as a whole, a palm and five functioning fingers. Now it seemed alien and alarming, something that had to be allowed and taken into account on its own. You sensed glimmers of joy and excitement at reopened possibilities, but at exactly that point you could not trust what was happening. Was the hand really returned, really alive? Or was this fitful self-delusion? As soon as you grasped the hand—or let it grasp you, let it stroke your face or rub your shoulder—would it go numb and limp and void? Would it prove again its real absence, the freshly crushing definitiveness of its loss?

That was what so disturbed Al about the dream. In it Valerie had appeared utterly, entirely alive. She looked and acted real apart from Al and Al's memories or fantasies. As he reviewed it dozens of times, he realized that in the dream Val had even aged slightly in the five years since he had last seen her. Or seen her like this, alive. Or, that is, *apparently* alive. That was the weirdness and craziness of the dream and its aftermath. He knew she was gone. How could there be any doubt about her death? And yet he now found himself thinking of her differently, in a way that not only reawakened old feelings, well-rehearsed memories, but also intimated the potential of new feelings, of making new memories with Valerie. That was impossible, absurd. Any such feelings or hopes, however tentative and evanescent, could only disappoint, and disappoint bitterly. Like the one-handed man who thought he sensed a tingling of life, Al shook it off. For safety and sanity's sake, he denied it. He distracted himself from awareness of it and forgot it.

At least, he tried to.

❧

Albert did much of his attempting to forget the dream on morning and evening commutes to and from Old Chicago. Walking to or away from the sub train station, he often fell into conversation with other pedestrians. But once they were aboard, the train's rhythmic motion and sounds seemed to silence and lull passengers into a trance, if not slumber. On this particular morning, Al's car included a mix of strange and familiar faces. Beside him sat an old man with an egregious comb-over. As the disheveled fellow nodded in and out of sleep, the lone lock of hair somehow stayed in a solid piece and swung like a scythe across his smooth pate. A man on the upper deck munched on a biscuit grasped in a crumpled paper bag. Two lovers at the front of the car faced Al, the man slouched with his legs flung wide, his arm casually laced around the woman. He monopolized the seat and probably, Al thought, the woman's entire existence. She was curled up compactly, with a tired and resigned look. Burbles of conversation flowed about the coach in three different languages. Some children chattered loudly.

Albert looked ahead to another day of the most lucrative—if not actually lavishly paying—job he'd ever held. He tutored teenaged heirs of the constituency, as the inner-city wealthy class was known. In the days of plentiful, affordable petroleum, now receding into the obscurity of the past, there had been a steady drift away from books and widespread basic mastery of the sciences. Reading and learning, after all, required patience and arduous discipline. Why seek information or entertainment by these time-consuming, often monotonous, means when they were otherwise instantly and easily accessible? Education and enjoyment via imagistic, computerized media appeared vastly superior in their efficiency.

During the ongoing decades of the Descent (so-called because it plunged society into the more spartan, demanding period after the "peak" availability of oil), the constituency hoarded not only economic power but the dwindling reserves of petroleum, alongside the consequent ready supply of electricity. Of course, without affordable energy, the panoply of electronic devices that functioned on it was useless. Laptop computers, cell phones, televisions, video game players, and portable music devices by the millions gathered dust in attics or rotted in landfills. Not all were laid aside, however. In Old Chicago and other major cities around the country, the constituency still enjoyed the generous (if decreased) availability of energy and electricity. Constituents continued to depend on electronic technology. As they shunned the burdens of reading and the sciences over generations, their skills in these areas atrophied and faded. But in recent years there were second thoughts. Was it really prudent, constituents asked themselves as political conflicts flared, to entrust all their technical support to the subs who so grossly outnumbered them? Also, the mass entertainment and arts industry had long ago become unaffordable and infeasible. Movies hadn't been made for decades; recorded and digitized music was a relic. Onerous as they had been, obsolete as they had become, traditional books reassumed value. Much of the constituency now wanted its young trained—for necessity and for pleasure—in literature and history, in math and the practical sciences.

That was why Albert rode the train six days a week: to ground constituent adolescents in what once had been known as the humanities, and teach them some basic algebra. Like Al, most tutors came from devout Christian or Jewish families. Poke McNearland, the longtime priest at St. Brendan's, offered the most succinct explanation for this reality that Al had ever heard. Father McNearland pointed out that, as their adherents understood them, Judaism and Christianity were not philosophies or abstract systems of thought. Neither were they folk religions based on the perennial, timeless cycle of the seasons and life and death. Instead, Jews and Christians rooted their faiths in particular stories from the past. God had revealed himself and his aims uniquely in the characters of Moses and Jesus, in the events of the exodus from Egypt and the crucifixion. In turn, these stories, and other texts radiating around them, were contained in Scripture. Thus Jews and Christians (along with Muslims) really were "people of the book." At least some of them must be able to read and continually refresh their communities of faith.

"Take it another step deeper, really deeper," McNearland said. "God as we know God acts through time and space. But God can't be contained in the world. You can't put God in a box, even the biggest box. God can't be captured on the surface of things, so we could say God is all depth. That's why the bush that draws Moses to itself doesn't only burn, but it speaks. It not only shows on the surface and by its appearances, it manifests from its depths."

Often when Poke got rolling with an enthusiastic exposition, his eyes brightened and he smiled as if surprised and delighted by his own words. At least outside the pulpit, he might also veer into the salty language of his working class heritage. That was the case on this occasion. McNearland continued: "Think of this—the Gospel of John informs us that Jesus Christ is at his highest, his most exalted, when he is dying on a cross. Now, just by appearances and on the surface of things, how can you see the crucified Jesus as exalted? Bullshit! This is a naked and broken man under torture, enduring a horror. To see Jesus exalted on the cross, you have to know the story before the story. You have to know about the history of Israel and its expectation of a suffering servant messiah, its trust that God can work through ugliness and patient endurance. And you have to know the story *after* the story, that the Christ dying on a cross will be resurrected from the dead, and in his resurrection vindicated by God as the true messiah."

"It is words," Father McNearland concluded, "words of story and remembrance, that not only describe the surface of things—which after all is often bleak as hell—but also point to a deeper dimension of God's will and intention, God's spirit."

With the muffled shrill of the train's throaty horn, Al returned to the surface of things, to his mundane commute. Brakes squealed and the train slowed to a stop at one more commuter station before its destination in downtown Old Chicago. Al's seatmate theatrically erected himself with a groan, as if standing up was almost a full day's labor, and exited the car. A few others also stepped down onto the station platform, while several more climbed on the train. A bell rang urgently. The lumbering string of coaches clunked, jerked, and shuddered like a huge dog shaking itself awake. The train gathered speed and regained its pace. Static crackled over the car's intercom. Al sat up straight, yawned to open his ears. It was time for the conductor to read the morning's news.

❧

The constituency funded and fueled the train lines not only for its transportation, but for the ready movement of subs to engineer and build, cook and clean, tutor its children, and perform other menial tasks. Both constituents and subs wanted regular news, and with electronic media largely defunct, packed trains provided a natural venue for broadcasting in the Age of the Descent. There were, of course, other and more informal means for the distribution of information. But the constituency owned the railroads and very much liked the idea of providing and overseeing the sole extant form of mass media.

Today the conductor-newscaster began, as usual, with the weather. Forecasting had actually improved in recent years. Many means of scientific forecasting remained, and the Descent had returned all the population—subs and rural denizens especially, but constituents too—closer to nature. Weathermen reincorporated "folk methods" that scrutinized the movement and other behavior of bird flocks, various burrowing animals, and the massive buffalo herds resurgent on the Great Plains.

After a terse summary of the weather, the newsreader moved on to an account of recent regional robberies, sex crimes, and homicides. Then came a smattering of foreign news, which, today as usually, amounted to indirect (or not so indirect) hints why listeners were so fortunate to live in Old America rather than anywhere else in the world. Next came vital information about crops and the conditions for other foodstuffs. This was the part of the newscast where passengers were most likely to participatively jeer, as with this morning's announcement of tomato rationing, or to cheer. And at this moment resounding clapping, foot-stomping, seatback-banging, and shouting greeted the excellent tidings that brewers had a temporary oversupply and beer prices would plummet tomorrow. The exuberant din drowned out not only the thumping and clacking of the train but the amplified voice of the reader. The newscaster shut up for a minute or two, until the enthusiastic approval wound down to an infrequent hoot. Finally the intercom crackled again. The newscaster spoke:

> And now, the Headline of the Day.
>
> Authorities announced this morning that Congress is repealing the National Anti-Natal Law. The repeal, proposed by President Willie Gleason, has been under debate for several months. The lifting of the NAN eliminates penalties for childbearing men and women under age twenty-eight.
>
> "My colleagues have acted wisely," said President Gleason, lauding approval of his proposal. "The anti-natal law may once have been necessary. It is no longer."

The newscaster went on quoting the President. There was some murmuring and rustling among the passengers, but nothing approaching the raucous outburst for falling beer prices. While subs despised the NAN Law, they remained aware that there were constituents on the train with them. Outward celebration over the death of this controversial law might endanger jobs, if not more.

The Anti-Natal measure was implemented fifteen years earlier, forbidding any Americans to birth children before both the mother and father were already well into their childbearing years. The official rationale for the law was conservational, to hold down population growth and ease the human burden on Earth. Al and the other subs knew that was true—after all, the law applied to the constituency, too—but they also knew ecological righteousness was hardly the sole motivator behind it. Constituents wanted to preserve available petroleum energy, of which they were the primary remaining users. They also (and perhaps mainly) hoped to depress the birthrate among subs.

The law's draconian penalties contributed to the spite for it: pregs, women under age twenty-eight who got pregnant, were sentenced to a minimum of eighteen months in prison; impregs, the males under twenty-eight who fathered their children, were liable to mandatory sterilization. But comparatively, that was just kindling in the burning hatred subs bore against the NAN policies. What fueled anger into an inferno of resentment was the law's uneven enforcement. Relying on connections and superior legal and political resources, constituents usually escaped these severe punishments. Subs, by contrast, rarely avoided them.

In this light, Albert and other subs on the train were suspicious as they heard the newsreader quote the president and enumerate the official reasons for striking the law from the books. Officially, NAN policies were "no longer necessary" because alternative forms of energy were successfully under development and because "the great citizens of Old America" would now voluntarily, as a patriotic duty, keep birthrates low. This official account did not acknowledge that anti-natal law had become unacceptably difficult and expensive to enforce. Resentment of the law approached explosive heights, and prison populations had soared to unmanageable levels.

Not wanting to make potential trouble for himself, Al kept a well-practiced poker face as he heard this news. But inwardly, he imagined an ugly, hateful beast going down, and tingles of glee danced up his spine. He had known several people hurt by the NAN law. Two male friends, convicted, penalized, and no longer able to produce children, were spurned from marriage. One was reasonably content with his bachelorhood, if prone to bursts of anger and the occasional drunken binge. The other bitterly and constantly yearned for a spouse and family he would never have. Then there was Sharon Lorebain, who lived down the street from Albert's boyhood home. Sharon had married when she was twenty-two and gotten pregnant a year or two later. A teenaged Al was walking down the street one morning when he saw Ms. Lorebain arrested, handcuffed wrists behind her back, screaming, stumbling, and being dragged across her yard. She disappeared from the neighborhood for several months. When she returned, she was pale and sullen. She never said if her offspring had been aborted or given out for adoption. She never said much of anything. Before long she and her husband separated, and now she lived alone, the hermit of Banneker Street, with dandelions and prairie grass obscuring her front door.

Then, of course, and damn it, Al thought of Valerie. He recalled how they had begun to talk of marriage. Each of them had been an only child, and both wanted two or three kids. Some day, they told each other. His father had often joked how easy it was to be an expert on childrearing until a child was born to you, and Al supposed he and Val had only ever thought of raising a family naively, with all the pristine wonder only the inexperienced and untried can enjoy. But he knew they had wanted children. He knew Val would have been a great mother. And he knew it would never be. She was gone, more cruelly lost to him and to the world than Sharon Lorebain reclused in the wasting house down the street.

Another commuter train roared on tracks parallel to Al's own and a just few feet away. An instant eclipse closed and darkened his world, followed immediately by the batting of shadows and light, the zoetropic blur of faces flitting by on the other train. Then, just as suddenly as it had come, the adjacent train passed. The sound faded to its earlier level, the air pressure dropped. Steady, unbroken sunlight reasserted itself and the visual horizon beyond his window expanded from two feet to a view across the street to a row of bungalows. It occurred to Albert that this violent and yet innocent passage must be something like the sensation of being born. He remembered a documentary film about childbirth he had once watched. He remembered the scene of a newborn shooting from its mother's womb. It slid in a gush out of the uterus and plopped into the waiting physician's hands. Stunned and blinking, the infant churned its fists and feet at the air, then expelled its first breath and realized that in this strange new medium it could make noise. The baby cried, and Al supposed the cry meant something like *I'm here. But where am I?*

3

After work, homeward bound, Al found himself still abuzz with the news about the repeal of the National Anti-Natal law. His was not a lone excitement. The repeal put subs in a condition to celebrate. And the drop in beer prices, starting tomorrow, meant that beverage budgets would stretch further this week. Weary with himself and the haunted, aching mood that had gripped him since the other night's dream about Val, Albert joined the parade of peers who marched off the train stop straight down the block into the Dog and Duck Inn. In the subs' neighborhoods, licensed taverns were allowed access to electricity four nights a week. The Dog and Duck was one of those, attracting customers not only for conviviality but for bright respite from the otherwise pitch-black night.

Ensconced at the bar, Al nursed a couple of lagers before he determined he would stay awhile. He ordered a grilled-cheese sandwich and a D & D Iced Tea (the house specialty was bourbon-enhanced). He joshed with a neighbor and Uncle Eddie, the bartender, about whether or not he should settle in for the entire evening. Abcess Excess, a leading Old Chicago–area purveyor of celibate porn punk, was scheduled for its first set around 9:30 or 10.

Pretty soon Uncle Eddie brought Al's sandwich, along with a sweating, ice-gorged pitcher to top off his drink. Four or five young constituents entered the Inn and took a table directly behind Albert's barstool. They betrayed their slumming, alien status by their overly rowdy conduct—they were trying too hard to act as if they comfortably belonged. On top of that, they were unusually and immaculately garbed, especially one in the orange, billowing robes of a Tibetan monk. Al had an immediate idea what they were up to. They fell into noisy conversation about Abcess Excess.

One started, "This band's music . . ."

"If music it can be called," Uncle Eddie mock-whispered across the bar to Al. The constituents heard but missed only a beat or two.

The first speaker sounded from beneath a bushy beard and a Castro cap. "This band's music," he resumed his declamation, "represents the proletariat's refusal to let its sexual vigor be tamed and co-opted by capitalism. It revels in sexuality but refuses to reproduce wage slaves for the exploitation of the owner-class."

A second speaker, dressed in a vested suit with a watch-chain and brandishing a huge cigar, demurred. "From my psychoanalytic perspective, celibate porn punk is a denial of sexuality," he said. "Like frightened grade-schoolers, Abcess Excess likes to talk about—or scream about—something it only vaguely understands and never experiences. People who will not copulate resist the biological imperative of reproduction. They are afraid of reproduction because it is untidy and unpredictable."

"On the contrary," bushy-beard parried, "celibate porn punk channels sexual energy into agitation for revolution. And revolution requires the ultimate courage."

"*Pferd hoden!*" spat back the cigar-fondler. "Celibate porn punkers fear having children because it reminds them they will die. Sex and death are always conjoined. Together they make the original two-backed monster, from which the likes of this band flees as if it was Frankenstein on a rampage."

Bushy-beard smiled in spite of himself. Albert was confirmed in his guess that the tablemates were playing hypocricket, a game recently popular with re-educated constituents just beyond their teens. In it callow nihilists impersonated proponents of various ideologies. The object was to stay in character all evening, or sometimes for weeks. Some devotees of the game argued that the true master of hypocricket was one who could switch from the imposture of one faith to another rapidly and serially, like a quick-change artist of the soul. Others insisted the real master of hypocricket was one immersed in character so long and so profoundly that loved ones began to despair that their original friend or family member might never re-emerge.

At this juncture the monkishly clad constituent intoned, "Sex and politics are both illusions. True salvation lies in detachment."

"Salvation lies in getting out of here!" a fourth and new speaker shouted, as if hysteria confirmed the veracity of his statement. He slammed a

Bible the size of a paving stone on the tabletop. "Whatever porn punk is, it is straight from the devil!"

The tablemates lurched into momentary silence. "Sheesh," said the pseudo-Viennese, tossing his cigar down beside the Bible. "You are so pitiful at this . . ."

"Well," the Bible-bearer whined, "why do I always have to be the fundamentalist?"

Their game derailed, the hypocrickets abandoned their characters. Just as people gathered over a mediocre meal resort to conversation comparing other, superior meals and restaurants, the deflated contestants turned to talk of exemplary games they had played on other occasions. This led to argument about who was the best hypocricket player in the game's history, which naturally complicated itself with debates concerning the criteria for determining the master player. The tablemates rehearsed the merits of quick-change hypocricket versus those of long-term, immersive hypocricket. The blazing orange constituent, whose costume made him look as if he might be the source of a thickening layer of cigarette smoke now hovering across the room, recalled an acquaintance who dressed and acted like a radical feminist for three months, then apparently came to believe the ideology she was parodying. It seemed to her that gender divisions invariably did empower males and subjugate females. She told her boyfriend that all male-female sex was rape, by definition, and kicked him out of her apartment. "The question is, was she still playing hypocricket any longer?" said the would-be Tibetan holy man. "If she came to believe the role she was playing, and even to live it out—I mean, she and Walt had been together for a couple of years—isn't she now really a radical feminist, instead of a hypocricket?"

The Bible-banger, who was much less excitable after being relieved of his fundamentalist impersonation, spoke pensively: "It shows you that hypocricket can be a dangerous game even if you're not playing a gangster or a Nazi spy. If you concentrate on it and keep at it, you might become the part you play." He shuddered.

"Then again," he brightened, "maybe she didn't really become a radical feminist. Maybe she really is a super, super dedicated player of the game. And maybe in a year or two she'll say, 'Just kidding! Fooled you all!'"

"And invite Walt back home?" bushy-beard muttered sarcastically. There was some tentative laughter around the table.

"Seriously," said the cigar-fondler, who now held a cigarette with a constant blue smokestream sucked upward into the Inn's pervasive cloud. "Seriously, he has a point. The greatest, the supreme player of immersive hypocricket, would be someone who assumed a role for years, for decades even. For a lifetime . . ."

"And then spoke from death," the false fundie caught on. "She'd say, 'Hey, those last twenty-five years? I wasn't really a radical feminist. I just got into the game.'"

"'And at least the game had meaning, gave me some kind of direction,'" the poseur-psychoanalyst ventriloquized on behalf of the hypothesized, not-so-genuinely-radical radical feminist.

"Exactly," the bogus Bible-banger said. "Somebody might act like a practicing Jew or a Blakean mystic or an advanced capitalist, build a life around the role, leave everybody wondering, or not leave 'em wondering—have everybody convinced. Then, only after death is the mask removed. They send a telemortal text: 'Gotcha!' The greatest hypocricket move ever. By the greatest hypocricket player who ever lived. And died."

"I never thought about the hypocricket and the telemort," mused orange boy. "But the telemort could take the game to a whole new level . . ."

❧

Al departed the bar soon after Abcess Excess launched its sonic assault. Within seconds, the band's thundering drums and crunching guitars breached even the strongest audio barricade—Albert saw Uncle Eddie screwing his spongy earplugs deeper inside his head. By the time Albert was a block away, he thought the booming music probably resembled what a countrysider heard when a nearby city was under artillery fire. "Only less melodic," Uncle Eddie would add.

On his walk home, Al considered the technology mentioned by the young constituents. The telemortal texter, purportedly a means of communicating with the dead, had been perfected about ten years previously. The machines required tremendous amounts of power, so only four or five major cities hosted them. The telemort located in Old Chicago rested on the upper floor of a skyscraper, at the base of A-framed solar panels that soared another four stories above it. When operating, the telemort drew power not only from batteries charged by the sun, but from diesel engines and towering wind turbines planted offshore in Lake Michigan. The rarity of telemorts, coupled with the expense of activating them, meant that access to a telemort was limited and expensive. So it was mostly constituents who could afford a telemort session. Some subs—Al was one of them—saved for years for a fifteen-minute opportunity to communicate with a deceased loved one.

However precious the resources spent, what the telemort users got for their money was a chance to sit at a computer keyboard high in the sky, behind floor-to-ceiling glass facing out over the apparently endless expanse of Lake Michigan. They typed a few sentences and, assisted by a technician, launched them into the ether. Then they waited for a response to be displayed, trailing behind a cursor blinking on the bathtub-sized monitor mounted in the floor just beyond their keyboard. It could be a lone individual staring down at the monitor. But many times it was an entire family, semi-circled around the monitor, holding their breath and hoping Grandpa or Grandma had greetings from the great beyond.

Sometimes no response appeared. (No refunds: you paid for the opportunity only to attempt communication.) Sometimes a response would furl out across the screen in a language unknown to the family watching over the monitor—English-speakers, for example, might witness a few sentences instantiated in Arabic or Mandarin. (These could be translated upon payment of an additional charge.) Very occasionally the response was entirely straightforward and representative of the nether communicator's style when he or she walked among the living. A deceased dyspeptic might complain, "Shit, I'm still tired." A skinflint auntie might reveal: "The bonds are buried thirty-five steps west of the chicken coop. Cash ONLY IF NEEDED." Most often the messages were cryptic, vague, or allusive, as in: "Make hay while the tide's out" or "Light, light, light . . ." or "It ain't so hot here" or "Dante was close."

At its inception, the telemort had been hailed as the invention that would end all religious and philosophical mysteries. It would determine whether or not there was life after death and, if so, its exact nature. Poke McNearland correctly predicted this would not be the case. "Look," he said. "Any message, even if it is a bona fide message from the dead, is still a message. It has to be interpreted. And where there's room for interpretin', there's room for arguin'." So, beyond basic questions of whether or not the telemort was a hoax and a con, various telemorted communiqués that were rapidly published were just as rapidly debated. One of the first published messages read, "Purge tory." While some insisted this was an anathema on all Anglophilic conservatives, others said it was a locational remark from a bad Catholic who couldn't spell. When telemort monitors remained blank, atheistic materialists said, "I told you so." When an ellipses blinked across a screen (". . ."), some Buddhists said it indicated the perfect dispassion of Nirvana, certain Hindus claimed it hinted that humans are drops in the vast ocean of being, and mystically inclined mathematicians said it represented infinity.

The double-jointed, circus-contortionist flexibility of language—even language ostensibly employed by the dead—was proven especially by the emergence of anagrammarians. Set up in storefronts and sidewalk booths in the vicinity of the skyscraper housing the telemort machinery, anagrammarians accepted fees to decipher the true (or at least more satisfying) meanings of freshly received telemort texts that were baffling or discouraging. A couple of sisters communing with their late mother were crushed to find her apparently as misanthropic in death as she had been in life. "Assholes leftover," her telemort text grumped. But an anagrammarian, assuring them their mother really had mellowed and grown altruistic in her post-mortem sojourn, re-sorted the letters of the message to divine the magnanimous maternal command, "Love others as self." A telemorting nephew considered himself much poorer in cash but no richer in wisdom after a late uncle texted "Bongo odd gut." Actually a profound theological affirmation, "No God but God," advised an enterprising anagrammarian. A newly married couple sought vocational advice from a beloved, gone-but-not-forgotten professor. "Gauge my wontons," replied the sagacious professor from his grave. Were they supposed to open a Chinese restaurant, featuring very accurately sized dumplings? This though neither had culinary expertise beyond egg scrambling, nor a predilection for precision? They drifted aimlessly and disconsolately for days, until a consulted anagrammarian disclosed the true meaning: "Go west, young man." Then they cheerfully packed for a move to Old California.

At this juncture in his ruminations, Albert arrived at his home. He stepped from the sidewalk onto the grass fronting the Church of St. Brendan the Wanderer. He leaned his wiry figure against the frame supporting the church sign. He looked up into the black sky punctured by the light of scattered stars. At the moment the stars appeared disarrayed, separate, each alone in a crowd. The skein of thoughts spooling through Al's mind unwound in a jumble of impressions about the telemort, about death and life and any communion there might be between the two. He felt a bit drunk.

He cocked his head back and shouted into the silence, “Bongo odd gut!” He waited for a reply.

Then he took a few deep breaths and cleared his skull. He evenly climbed the stairs to the door opening into his apartment. Before he reached for the knob he saw an envelope taped to the door. “Albert—URGENT” was written on the outside of the envelope. He immediately recognized his mother’s handwriting. She was not a woman given to dramatic flourishes. Al tore the message off the door and scrambled inside. In seconds he had a lantern aglow. Still on his feet, he read:

> Dear Albert: I did not find you at home. Please come to me tomorrow. In light of recent events, I have much to tell you. To be honest, I have something to tell you and much to explain. Don’t be anxious, I don’t mean to alarm you. But we need to talk.
>
> Now as always, with love, Mother

As his heartbeat accelerated, Al chuckled. Whatever was to be made about the veracity and meaning of telemort texts, there was no doubt about this message. He had a sense that his life was about to change, radically, irrevocably. He looked back at the door and saw that he had left it wide open.

4

He touched Val the first time they met. It was a January morning. Snow blanketed the ground, its stunning whiteness broken only here and there, by the russet yellow ribbons of dog markings. Ice encased trees. When glittering limbs clattered in the wind, the air echoed with a sound like tackle tinkling against the aluminum masts of harbored yachts. He was on an errand and tried to hustle. But the sidewalks and streets were treacherously slick, so slick it seemed that if you fell you might slide clear off the face of the earth. These conditions forced him into a halting, uneven gait, with his arms spasming out for balance each time he slipped. Which he did frequently. Still, he was not self-conscious until he was six or seven blocks from his home and saw her stepping onto the front stoop of a brick bungalow.

She wore woolen pants and a white, waist-length down coat. Her brunette hair flowed luxuriously out from under a red and yellow striped stocking cap. It was the hair he noticed first. Then he took in her long legs. Suddenly he caught himself trying to walk normally, at a casual gait with his hands relaxed at his hips. *You idiot,* he thought. *You're twenty-five years old, not a middle schooler who's just realizing it might be more rewarding to impress girls than pester them.* They nearly intersected as she attained the sidewalk. Then she surged ahead of him at a quick pace that would have been natural and sustainable on dry ground. He knew how slippery the surface was, and that she operated unawares. He stretched strides to close the distance between them, trying to imagine how he might tactfully suggest that she slow down and take care. He was nearly even with her elbow when one leg jackknifed out from under her. She tipped backward and righted herself, barely, with a jerking forward over-correction. Now her feet scooted backward and she began to fall facedown. He got a grip on her churning elbow and pulled her up straight. In the instant that she recovered her footing, he lost his. Levering her upright rocked him off balance. His feet flung forward as if they were taking flight from the rest of his body. Instantaneously, without time even to flail, he was on his back.

She looked down at him with wide-open green eyes, gasping alluringly feminine sounds of concern and alarm. At impact his cap had shot off his head like cannon-fire. He lay below her bareheaded, his feet still held off the ground. His body was unhurt; his pride, decimated. Ridiculous figure that he was, what had he to lose now? His spirit felt buoyant, unbound from the merciless gravity that had thrown him on his back. A smile rose to his lips. He looked her in the eyes and heard himself say, "Such is the state of chivalry in the Age of the Descent."

And they laughed, together.

❧

Next their paths crossed at the train station. She sat on the bench with a beaten up paperback copy of *East of Eden* on her lap. They remembered each other's names, and smiled about the Chaplinesque aspect of their first meeting. He told her how much he liked Steinbeck and she went through her personal ratings of the author's canon: *East of Eden* in the lead, with *The Grapes of Wrath* second, then the others following in a blanket-finish. Except for *Tortilla Flat,* which left her cold; it seemed that Steinbeck wanted to make the paisanos sympathetic, but had managed only to show them comic at best and pathetic at worst. Directly he and she agreed to sit together on the train ride to Old Chicago. They both loved books, and with that mutual love a bridge sprung up between them. This, their first real conversation, was effortlessly rich and resonant. He reveled not only in her words but in her lilting soprano voice and her brilliant smile, which burst into view repeatedly. She liked his ready sense of humor, his unusual but not grating laugh. For emphasis of a point, she at one moment lightly poked and tapped his upper arm. To him it was as if she were gingerly testing a stovetop pan or pot, making sure it was not too hot to touch. The small gesture captivated him. Before they left the train, they had planned a date.

Over subsequent months they went downtown and walked the shores of Lake Michigan. They watched neighborhood softball games and flew kites and met at each other's home to eat together and play board games. They taught each other favorite songs. They took turns reading aloud all manner of books—Augustine's *Confessions* and Kierkegaard and Michel Serres and *A Prayer for Owen Meany.* Every occasion, whatever else it involved, was an opportunity to talk and to listen, to learn more about the other, sometimes in sips and sometimes in gulps, but never with the thirst for their company slaked. For each of them the other was a new world to be explored, brimming with wonders and some dangers (those helped keep you alert). After a few months it seemed that there was nothing either would hide from the other. They related not only triumphs and amusing foibles, but what they considered the darkest, most shameful parts of themselves. They learned to be confident in their them-ness as a single planet securely encompassing both their worlds, both their lives past and to come. The only passion neither could evoke in the other was humiliation or embarrassment.

Naturally their spiritual and emotional intimacy was accompanied by physical intimacy. At first they simply learned how to fit each other's lips together, keeping noses out of the way. But since they found each other's outer selves as endlessly fascinating as their inner selves, their bodily explorations advanced quickly. One summer night she arrived at his place in cutoff jean shorts and a T-shirt. A lean woman in cutoffs was irresistible to him. They were on the couch, necking, before she had time to ask for the glass of water she needed after her walk from across the neighborhood. He caressed her rump and thighs as his tongue slid into her ear. Wait a minute—he felt goosebumps, but only on one leg. A probing tongue in her right ear raised bumps on her right leg, though not the left. He kissed across her face, grazing her cheek, the tip of her nose, her lips, the other cheek, then slyly flicked his tongue in her left ear. Now there were goosebumps on her left leg, though not the right. For the next five minutes he delectably repeated the experiment. The hypothesis was validated, and with amused pleasure he informed her of his discovery.

"Wow," she said. "You're teaching me things about myself that I never knew."

"A sweet victory of the scientific method," he humbly demurred.

This was a woman and a man in their mid-twenties, playing as grown-ups do. Yet though they were not ashamed or feeling guilty, a shadow hung over their sexual activities. That shadow was the National Anti-Natal Law. If she were to become pregnant, the baby would be removed from them and they both would suffer penalties. Certainly they would be separated, which itself would be an unbearable punishment. So they took precautions.

Their parents, at first encouraging of their relationship, had grown cooler on it as it became apparent how serious the two were about one another. They took occasion to remind their adult children, not always subtly, about the NAN laws and the fact that subordinates—unlike constituents—always suffered their consequences. Eventually, his father became especially insistent that the two should, as he put it, "slow down." Then one night they dropped by her parents' house and found his father there. What was he doing? The parents were briefly sheepish, blushing and clearly caught in the act of something. They quickly picked up the bobbled ball of their conversation and put it back into play. But he had taken note, and at the end of the evening he followed his father out the door. As they walked together, he queried about what his father and her parents had discussed before their children arrived. He learned that his father was pressing with her parents the case that the two of them should "take a break," and maybe resume their friendship in few years, when both were at least twenty-eight years old.

He was outraged at his father's meddling. He wanted a promise that his father would drop the suit against their relationship, and never again present it to her parents. His father stalled and attempted to divert the discussion from any such vow. The heights of the son's sense of injustice then rose, and it was from atop a wall of righteous anger that he threw down an ultimatum. He demanded that his father *immediately* promise to desist, or else the son would quit not his relationship with his lover, but his relationship with his father. In quiet but unrepentant sorrow, the elder responded that the younger couple's love was a fine thing in itself and at the same time too hazardous to continue. "Then that's it. It's decided," the son said. And he stalked away from his father into the night, until darkness obscured each from the other's sight.

The following day he and Val were alone, in his apartment. They lay together on his bed, in the big cave at the end of the long, tunneling flat. An early fall breeze blew through the open windows at the front of the apartment. The yellowed trees rocked their boughs gently. They rested in each other's arms. She told of her disappointment with her parents, and he told her about the confrontation and then the break with his father. She wept. Then they were kissing and embracing desperately. Clothes came off as if of their own volition. At some point they were both naked. This was the point when they normally paused and saw to their precautions.

But now, in the swirl of anger and desire, he wanted nothing between them. Nothing—no parent, no law, no withholding thin skin—nothing could keep them apart, not by a millimeter or a million miles. She was no less caught up in desire than he, but not so angry. There was a moment when she started to say something, but then his hips were cradled by her opened legs, and she could not and did not want to stop it. For months and years later he would look back on that first instant when he was fully inside her. He would want to forget it, but he knew that at that moment he felt an onrushing ecstasy and yet held back a piece of himself, reserving it for anger, for spite of his father. The ecstasy rolled, gained momentum, then crested and broke over him like a wave. It washed away the anger and engulfed him in the love he shared with this woman. But still, it was clear and undeniable that he had interrupted their fusing and tainted it with the dishonoring of his father.

What was it about a man, he wondered as she drifted off in a nap, that made him turn love against love, working death in himself by that which is good? He decided he should not completely trust himself. He turned to her with a resolve to build and fashion a love that was pure, that did not rely on spite or hatefulness or any kind of exclusion for its definition and animation. He reclaimed her and them on the basis of this resolution, poised like a marathon runner with eyes on the distant goal of pure love.

❧

But then, barely two months later, she was gone. That was what people said about people who had died. They were "passed away," "departed," "no longer with us"—in short, finally and irrevocably "gone." His life, like a calendar hinged on the advent of a new millennium, pivoted on this before and after. The before was when she was not gone. Those were the days when it was not too hard, usually, to imagine God smiling on creation: in spring sunshine, in soft rains, in the raucous play of children and the full gallop of a fine horse. The after was when she was and would always be gone. In the after he was numb to the surrounding world, rain or shine, imploded into the black hole of himself. His laughter, when it came, rang hollow to his own ears. Eventually he forgot how to cry. For all he would let anything touch or move him, he might as well have been walking about in an astronaut's suit. He imagined exactly that sometimes. Helmeted and carapaced, he was insulated, invulnerable to whatever toxicity (or perfume) other people released into the atmosphere he did not share. He breathed in only the fumes of his private despair. Like a floating spaceman, he drifted along on the momentum built up in the before part of his life.

Here was the bitter story Val's parents told: With them, she had gone downstate to visit her cousins. One warm but not too hot afternoon, the cousins decided to hike a nearby riverside forest. It was a beautiful place, with impressive draws cut into limestone, their walls glowing with an emerald light filtered through the foliage of trees and vines. A well-worn trail led by these small canyons, then climbed up and up, until green gave way to blue and you burst out atop towering cliffs. Far below coursed the river. Like a placid beast of burden, it carried felled trees and resting waterfowl and massive barges. In the air above it, hawks spiraled high on thermal currents. As cozy and secure as a forest might be, there was something liberating about working your way through a dense enclosure of woods, onto a promontory from which you could see as far as forever.

Maybe it was this sudden and exhilarating sense of freedom, they said, that impelled Val to venture out on the edge of the cliff. In all events, she was nearer the rocky cusp than either of her cousins. Then the soft stone crumbled and broke away, and just like that she disappeared. Or, to be more precise about how the witnesses put it, she was "gone." Reluctant to move any closer to the cliff's edge, the pair of cousins shouted out her name. Only echoes of their own calls returned to them. Eventually one cousin made brave and crawled, then wriggled on her stomach, so that she could look over the drop. All the long way down, plunging into greenery below, she saw no sign of her disappeared relative. She returned to her sister's side, then the two retreated hastily back the way they had come. They breathlessly accosted a ranger at the park's lodge office. The ranger questioned the panicked cousins, then enlisted a colleague for the rescue.

Her body was found two hundred feet below the point where it fell. It had struck at least two abutments on its drop. That and unyielding tree branches, to say nothing of the force of final impact, had horribly bent and mangled her. Three hours later police escorted her father to the mortuary. He came back out in shambles, a much older man than he was when he entered. His daughter's broken body and ruined face were so horrible he advised his wife against viewing it. She had never seen her husband so ravaged, and finally she relented. Since they were forgoing an open-casket funeral, they had her cremated in the downstate mortuary. They returned home a week later, bearing their only child in an urn.

At her interment her ashes, safe within a toy-sized and ornate casket, were reverently placed in a hole three feet deep. A few of the bereaved, those closest to her, grimly formed in a single file line for a turn at dropping a handful of soil into the grave. Al, still shell-shocked from the news of her death, stood in line behind her parents. For several excruciating moments, her father and mother awkwardly looked at each other. Neither wanted to commit the terribly final act of beginning to close the grave. Then her mother stepped forward brusquely, knelt on both knees, and scooped at the small earthen pile. She managed to grasp a fistful of soil and move her hand above the hole, but then her hand would not open and release the dirt. She breathed deeply and stifled her sobs. She bent down, her arm extending in the grave until her knuckles brushed her daughter's casket. Then she opened her hand, withdrew her arm, and struggled to her feet, with a relative sidling up to assist her.

Next her father dragged himself forward, as if to his own execution. He took hold of a couple of clods and straightened up over the grave. His hand trembled, so violently that the clods jostled and crumbled in his loosely closed fingers, sifting out beside the grave as much as into it. "Oh, Jesus!" he cried out. Solicitous relatives helped him move again.

It was Al's turn next. He sympathized with her parents. But he was numb, chronically stunned, not quite believing she was really dead, really gone. Let this be one of our lighthearted games, he thought, a kind of hide-and-seek in which he actually knew exactly where she was secluded but bumbled around as if he were clueless. Complete the ritual with the dirt, so as to be released and go to find her, to talk to her and listen to her and take her in his arms. In this state, he was able to perfunctorily enact his duty. He dropped soil into the grave, glancing at and away from the golden box at its bottom. *Now I've completed the count: ready or not, girl, here I come!* He staggered away from the graveside.

And he kept staggering, wandering in a daze for a week or two, half expecting her to bound off a car at the train stop or knock on his door some evening when the summer light had gone buttery and enshrouded everything in a tender veil. But he couldn't find her or be found by her, and gradually grew tired and then frustrated with the game. *Okay. I give up. Come out, come out wherever you are.* And still she made no appearances. For several days he was flooded with unbearable anxiety, trying not to remember the funeral, the thing with the dirt, fighting and pushing it all back with memories of her pert nose, her so-alive eyes, her cinnamon-freckled breasts, her touch and embrace.

Then he was worn down and overcome. Frighteningly, bitterly, it was getting harder and harder to remember her as she was, in all her spiritual and physical vitality. More and more he could only think of her as dusty ashes and shards of incinerated bones. He could not find her, he could not recover her, in any other form. Only then, tortured beyond his endurance, could he admit to himself that she had passed away, she had departed, that she was no longer with him or anyone else on the face of the earth. She was, oh no-no-no-no but yes, *gone.*

5

"I have much to tell you," Albert's mother had written. "To be honest, I have something to tell you and much to explain . . ."

Albert had reread the note so many times he had it memorized. After discovering it and first reading it, he had somehow fallen asleep quickly. But he woke a few hours later, in the dead of night, after the alcohol's effects had worn off. He ignited a candle and lay studying the message. She urgently wanted to see him. She wrote "in light of recent events." He reasoned that his mother's note, and the further information she had to convey, had something to do with the repeal of the National Anti-Natal Law. That was, after all, the most significant event of recent days. But then there was her confessional tone—"something to tell you and much to explain." How could his mother be implicated in any of the woeful effects of that dark law? And what about such inconceivable complicity could cause Mother to owe *him* an explanation?

Mother Simmel, now in her mid-sixties, was a woman of indomitable character. Like Ray Simmel, she was a member of the generation that came to maturity in the early decades of the Age of the Descent. The parents of this generation had learned through hard experience that surviving in the new world, the world after cheap petroleum, would mean living without the vast array of creature comforts taken for granted before the Descent. Heat or refrigerated air with the flick of a switch, abundant food with no more effort than it took to lift hamburger from a supermarket freezer, frequent long-distance travel, endless hours of diversion via laptops or smart phones—all these were pleasures and securities no longer available, especially to subordinates. Ray and Alva Simmel grew up soaking in the common sub wisdom that the affluent inhabitants of the Western world during the twentieth and the early twenty-first centuries were both scoundrels and wastrels.

A century and a half was a short period in the span of human history. And in that brief interval the privileged masses had squandered fossil fuels that geology built up over millions of years. The squandrels (as these privileged masses came to be known during the childhoods of the elder Simmels) not only eviscerated the earth's carbon-based guts but mowed down old-growth forests, decimated entire animal species, poked holes in earth's atmosphere, and spoiled immense oceans with their garbage. It was as if reckless and hateful children threw a party and, once started, would not stop until they had destroyed the home that so generously enabled their revelry. They tore stuffing from all the furniture, filled bedrooms with trash, ripped up the floor and dug into the ground beneath it, heaping dirt throughout the house. They gouged light fixtures from the ceiling and overturned bookshelves and clogged the toilets and broke all the windows. Finally, when they had exhausted themselves and the creation that sustained them, when they had wasted what forebears handed down to them and cheated future ancestors out of their share, they called an end to the party. They and their likes died off without shame, pining for the profligate golden age and assuming, with the bitter pride of the frightened and angry elderly, that they had seen human civilization reach its summit. All that awaited the human race in their wake was reduction, diminishment, and humiliation.

So Ray and Alva Simmel were taught. With the squandrels as a moral foil, Ray and Alva and their peers learned to honor toughness and a self-sufficiency accompanied by concern for your neighbors' welfare. They prized loyalty and living lightly on the earth. It was clear they would never have much, by way of money or material goods, to hand on to their heirs, so they expected the most valuable bequest they could leave their children was a good name and some semblance of a sustainable world.

Trying to fathom the motives of his mother's note via what he knew of her character, Albert lay under candlelight until dawn's first light was announced by noisy birdcalls in the trees just outside his window. He rose at 5:30 and set to work on assignments for his tutelary charges. Bulking up his students' homework would allow him to depart them early, and arrive sooner at the meeting with his mother.

Al arrived in the city and attended to his tutoring duties. Then, the workday behind him, Al trained out of the city toward Mother Simmel's neighborhood. Anxious and again attempting to divine the intent of her meeting, he found only bafflement. But reminiscence on her flinty and colorful character brought to mind one of his favorite incidents from her life, and he decided to indulge the memory of it as a diversion from the frustration at the failed anticipation of what his mother might have to tell him.

The incident had occurred in the third year of Alva's widowhood. She had grieved Ray Simmel severely and, though she refused to move in with her son or close friends, admitted she was terribly lonely. To occupy herself across empty days, she enlarged her garden and, in season, spent many of her daylight hours seeding, cultivating, watering, and harvesting. In late fall and winter she knitted, endlessly supplying neighbors and their children with caps, sweaters, stockings, and blankets. She remained active with her church, but otherwise curtailed her social life. Then she began regular visits to and from a widower neighbor, Harold "Corky" Angleton. Alva had known Corky for years and always enjoyed his company. But now, in the changed marital circumstances of their lives, mild amusement and appreciation morphed into infatuation. It had been decades, a lifetime, since Alva had been "in love," and she had thought the capability for it had passed with her youth. How was it, then, that she once more felt her heart leap when she heard a man's voice, and focused on this man with her last conscious thought every night and her first thought every morning?

Corky himself was a bit of a bon vivant, overflowing with stories and a knack for turning the most mundane chore into a small adventure. Corky and Alva were both healthy and energetic, though each one had a significant handicap. For Corky, it was his eyesight—he was basically blind, sojourning now in a world of shadows and dim lights. For Alva, it was her hearing—she struggled to sustain conversation through a sonic murkiness of dull plinks and echoes, as if she were underwater. Typically, though, the couple suffered their impairments with humor, suggesting that with Alva's eyesight and Corky's hearing, they could get on just fine.

The most pleasing proof of their elegant complementarity occurred one evening in Albert's presence. He, Corky, and his mother were dining at a restaurant when a tall, grandly stomached gentleman ambled up to the table and talked, familiarly, with Corky and Alva. It was clear from the gentleman's demeanor and address—he called them "Corky" and "Alva"—that he knew them well. And that they should know him. But after a few minutes, it was just as clear to Albert that neither his mother nor Corky were sure who was visiting with them. Their laughter was forced, their agreement with his suggestions cautiously delayed, then greeted with over-eager enthusiasm once the suggestions appeared innocuous. If the visitor detected their struggle at recognition, he betrayed no hint of the detection. After five minutes he departed as amiably as he had arrived. Corky held his tongue until the gentleman's voice faded into the distance, then he queried Alva: "Who was that man? What did he look like?"

"I don't know," she responded. "What did he say?"

It said much about Mother Simmel that she never complained about her ailments or limitations, that she laughed delightedly at her foibles when Al retold this and similar anecdotes. He loved her not least for her courage, for her strength in weakness.

Alva Simmel ushered her son into her cozy apartment with maternal enthusiasm. Her head came no higher than his shoulder, and he braced himself for her hug—which was always accompanied by stinging slaps on his kidneys. After the painful administration of her affection, he unstiffened and kissed her on the forehead. She clucked approval. He could restrain himself no longer, and burst out, "Mother, what's going on?" She took a step backward. It was her turn to stiffen. Recovering her sense of command, she ordered him to a seat in her parlor. She insisted that she prepare cups of tea before they began their talk.

Al seated himself on the front edge of a floral-printed couch. He heard her knocking about in the kitchen, occasionally sending forth perfunctory inquiries about his work, or comments on the weather. Al basically grunted in reply. He tried sitting back and relaxing, but within moments found himself scooted forward onto the edge of couch.

Portraits of his father and grandparents adorned the walls of the room. The fireplace mantle was lined from one end to the other with giraffe figurines. Most gamboled on all four legs, trailed by their youngsters hobbling along on splayed legs. A separate giraffe whimsically sat on the front edge of the mantle, with its back legs hanging over and its front hooves grasping a rolled-up newspaper. A couple wore Christmas caps, bright red with white balls at their tips. His mother said she loved giraffes for their sheer unlikeliness—who would think such gangly limbs and craning necks could hold a creature upright, let alone propel it across plains and set it feeding in treetops? But more than that, she said, she liked giraffes because they could see farther than any other earthbound animal.

Alva re-entered the room with a full platter, moving guardedly, with some of the jerky locomotion of her mascot animal. She placed the platter on a coffee table between her chair and Albert's spot on the couch. She dropped a sugar cube into her cup, then poured milk into Al's, handing it to him atop a saucer. She sipped at her tea, gingerly, and Al felt vaguely, oddly sorry for her. He looked across the table at her silver helmet of closely cropped hair. She seemed unaccountably old and tired. He noticed how she was stooped, her chin drooping on her collarbone, her shoulders curled in toward her sternum. It appeared as if her body was caving in on itself.

His discomfort grew. He started, "Mother . . ."

She interrupted him with a rush of words: "So, you have heard about the Anti-Natal Law? About its repeal?"

He sipped on the hot tea to calm himself, to gain patience. Then: "Yes. I have."

"It's such a cliché," she went on, "but I don't know how to say it, how to tell you this."

"Tell me what?"

"Oh, dear Lord. I've thought it over for hours . . . and I'm, I'm still at a loss. So I will just spit it out, and we'll go from there. But first," and here she resumed looking directly at him. "First of all, you know that your father loved you very much. And I love you very much. You know this? Yes?"

Al was confused. She paused as if she genuinely expected an answer. He gave it. "Of course I know that. Dad and I had our problems, but I never thought for a moment that he stopped loving me. And I know you love me. I know that, Mother."

"Good, that's good. Now remember that . . ."

"Mom, you're scaring me," he interrupted. "Like you say: just spit it out."

"All right. Yes. Here is the crucial point. Valerie is probably alive."

Al's mouth went dry, instantly. The room fell silent. The table fan running in the kitchen was audible. Al heard a clinking noise, then realized that his hand was trembling, shaking the teacup on its saucer. He sat the cup and saucer down.

"Valerie? Alive? *Probably* alive? What in God's name are you saying?"

"All right. Let me talk. Let me spill it all out, as best I can. Then you can ask questions. You were not told, but Valerie was . . . was pregnant. She was with child, with your child. Your father and I and the Harmons—Mr. Harmon came to us right after Valerie gave him the news. We didn't know what to do. But we knew that ugly, horrible law would mean not only the death, or at least the loss to us, of our grandchild . . . It meant not only that, but that you and Valerie would be punished, even have your lives ruined."

Al reeled. The questions and emotions proliferated and tumbled in his mind. He seized one: "How could I not have been told? That Val was pregnant? That she—that I—was going to have a child?"

Mother Simmel sighed. "She wanted to tell you. But we, I mean the Harmons and your father and I, we persuaded her to hold off, to wait until there was no doubt about the pregnancy. They had their trip downstate planned. Mr. Harmon had a friend, a physician-friend, down there. They'd been close since they were children together. They knew they could trust this doctor to check over Val and keep her condition quiet. Once they were there, and her pregnancy was confirmed, we had a plan to set in motion.

"The Harmons spent days convincing Valerie that she had to flee, to hide herself, and eventually the baby, away from the constituency and the authorities. She had to do it for you and for the baby. You and she could not disappear at the same time, or the police would have been suspicious. They would have set out after both of you. And we needed some way to make it seem as if the authorities didn't even need to look for Valerie. We enlisted the help of two more of Mr. Harmon's trustworthy friends, the park ranger and the mortician. We faked Valerie's death. God help us, we faked her funeral."

Al swam up out of an overwhelmed state and spoke numbly. "The Harmons were wrecks at the funeral. And you're telling me they were just acting?"

"In a way they were. But in a way they weren't. They sent her away. For all they knew, they might never see her again in their lifetimes. And that turned out to be the case, as you know. They're both gone now. So they had plenty to mourn and grieve. Added to that was the burden of guilt. I'm not asking you to feel sorry for us, Albert, but the Harmons and we could hardly stand deceiving our friends and neighbors. And we could just barely stand the guilt of seeing you in such pain, and not saying anything. But we knew that if we did you'd go after her."

She wept quietly. There is a cruel quirk of human nature, one that can cause us to hold fire with our temper until a loved one shows vulnerability, then to release and spew pent-up anger when a child or a brother or a parent drops the shield and admits her wrong.

"Damn it, Mother," Al said through clinched teeth. "We weren't children. I wasn't a child."

"Yes, son. I know. We knew. And I can't begin to tell you how it tore me up, how it tore your father up, when you and he had fought and were . . . apart. He knew that if he ever talked to you and admitted what we'd done, then you might never forgive him. There were times, after she was gone, when you thought he was distant out of stubbornness and pride. But it wasn't pride. He knew that if he talked further to you, he'd be sorely tempted to confess, to admit what he'd done, what we'd done, and tell you Valerie was still alive."

At the reintroduction of Valerie's name, Al felt the anger abate. He stepped back and saw himself so unbecoming, seething at his mother, and he stopped seething. He sensed in himself, like distant water thundering down a parched channel, something he had not sensed for a long time. It was hope. The National Anti-Natal law was dead and gone. But Valerie was alive, at least so far as his mother knew. What joy flooded him, overwhelming the other, conflicting emotions he felt in this sudden vortex he was plunged into. It already seemed almost a reunion, just knowing that she had not died, that somewhere she breathed air and walked the face of this earth. He imagined her, green eyes still glowing, bright smile still bursting forth, hair still swaying, lifted by a breeze. He wanted to laugh and to cry in relief. He and Valerie—and a child, *their* child—could be reunited. He looked his mother in the eye and committed himself to beginning to forgive her. He spoke calmly: "There is so much I want to know, Mother. But tell me now about Valerie. Tell me about Val and how I can get to her. Tell me how I can find her and bring her home."

6

It was like falling in love all over again. It took three days, and many more conversations with his mother, before Al really believed Valerie was alive. Al found the complexion of his existence changed. After the melancholic years of Val's supposed death, Al's prayers shifted from pleas for perseverance and faith in a gray world, to ecstatic thanksgivings. Val's own faith, deep and steady, had helped him hold on to his, sometimes by the fingernails. It was something he held in common with her, something of her he had not lost. And it also held out the hope of resurrection from the dead, and what had been his only prospect of meeting Val again. Now, in the early days after Mother's monumental confession, it was springtime, and for the first spring in many years, Al watched trees grow heavy green canopies and heard creeks thaw and surge from trickles to full flows, and he felt like he was a part of the natural festival of new life. He did not look on dully, removed and insulated, but sensed his heart lifting with the temperatures. The brooding shadows evaporated from his consciousness. He repeatedly awakened in the nights, momentarily heavy and blurry. But then in a split second, like an unwinding film jumping back onto its sprockets, everything became focused and bright, and he recalled the changed circumstances of his existence. She was alive! Alive and out there, somewhere, waiting for him. He slept in starts and stops, out of excitement, and still enjoyed an abundance of daytime energy.

He needed the energy. There were many preparations to make before he departed. He had to arrange replacement tutors for his students, since he would be absent at least three or four months. And he needed to embark within weeks—a long overland trip would be all the harder and more perilous during a Midwestern winter. So he immediately began to attend to the travel planning and gathering of supplies and equipment. The trip would be perilous enough without severe weather. He was venturing into territory filled with dangers, both human and natural. There was, furthermore, no guarantee he would succeed in finding Valerie. But that was a thought he chased from his mind.

If Al needed to see to his preparations, Mother Simmel's immediate duty was one of the most difficult she had ever undertaken. But two days after she had revealed the true nature of Valerie's disappearance to Al, she shouldered her responsibility and proceeded to Father McNearland's office. She confessed that she—along with her now deceased husband and the late Harmon parents—had deceived Father McNearland and their church. The cleric steepled his fingers and listened intently to Alva Simmel's story, prodding her onward with an occasional "I see" or a low hum. Eventually he asked some questions to get straight on some details. Then he asked her how she would like best to handle this with the parish. After discussion, the two agreed that Father McNearland would quietly spread the word of Valerie's—well, non-death—throughout his parish. And then, at a commissioning service for sending Albert on his travels, Alva would address the entire congregation. Father McNearland said a prayer for Alva, for Al and Val, for the steadiness and gentleness of their entire church. When Mother Simmel rose to leave, she thanked the priest and then put an observation of her own: "You know, you really don't seem all that shocked or surprised about this."

Father McNearland looked her in the eyes. "I will only say that I wondered, Alva. But sometimes it is best that the shepherd avert his eyes, and not know everything his flock is doing." Then he winked. Later Mother Simmel said that wink lifted her guilt and freed her spirit more than any formal pastoral absolution ever could have done.

❧

Despite his misgivings about the despair he suffered on false pretenses, Al had to admit that Valerie had been ingeniously spirited to safety. His mother explained that Valerie was smuggled well away from Old Chicago via a chain of churches linked by what was known as the Romans 16 Network. In the Age of the Descent, the Christian church had dwindled among the constituency. Among subordinates, however, the church had remained vital and renewed forms of survival and association rather like those the earliest church relied on amid a not always friendly Roman Empire. Bereft of personal wealth and the ministrations of the welfare state or behemoth insurance companies, the subs built instruments of health care and family aid in and through their churches. The Romans 16 Network was one of those instruments.

Named after the salutations the Apostle Paul addressed to a series of Christians and house churches in the last chapter of his Letter to the Romans, the Network loosely connected churches across the Old United States. It was subtle and shrewd, since it sometimes needed to operate without notice by the constituency and its government—as in cases such as Valerie's untimely pregnancy. Al was informed that members could make themselves known to one another by inquiring with words lifted from the closing verses of Romans chapter 16. "Praise God who strengthens us according to the gospel and proclamation of Jesus," was the opening code. The response signaling recognition and ready confederacy came from the second part of this doxology, "According to the revelation of the mystery that was kept secret for long ages."

By this process, Valerie was first shuttled across Lake Michigan by a member of the Network. Then, on the eastern shore of the lake, she was put into the hands of another member, who moved her again some distance, and entrusted her to yet another member of the Network. This process was repeated several times, until she was accepted into the haven of church quite distant from her home of Old Chicago. Each link in the human chain of the Network knew only two other links in that chain—the link who had brought Valerie to him or her, and the link to whom she had been handed on in turn. This meant that Mother Simmel had no idea where Val now resided. It entailed that Albert could find her only by following from one link of the chain to the next. It further entailed that his travel must largely be improvisational, and that he would have to depend in no small part on the hospitality of churches along the way.

That was why Father McNearland joshed, "This journey may make a Christian out of you, Al. Maybe none of us are really Christians until we are forced to resort to prayer and rely on one another." McNearland reminded Al of Jesus' exhortation to his followers to be shrewd as serpents and innocent as doves. "Follow that maxim, son. Damn! I suppose the trick is knowing when to be a snake and when to be a dove." Then his smile faded and he stared into the distance and murmured, "I do like the prospect of seeing Valerie again."

St. Brendan the Wanderer's church filled for the commissioning service that would send Al on his way. Nearly two hundred souls had squeezed into the pews and even occupied the choir stall. Father McNearland had charged Al with the liturgical reading of the Scripture lessons for the day, so Al sat in a chair on the east side of the altar railing, next to the priest, and looked out on all the faces of those attending. These were the people he shared the Eucharist with every week, becoming with them the body of Christ. He saw the now elderly men and women who had taught him in Sunday school. He caught the beaming smiles of his godparents, who had seen him baptized. Every direction he looked there were people who had helped him with schooling and hobbies, taken him to summer camps in Old Wisconsin, eaten and wept with him and his mother on the occasion of Ray Simmel's death, celebrated his accomplishments large or small. He looked out over the congregation and saw men who believed for him when he could not believe, women who prayed in his stead when he was empty of words or hope. He saw those he had grown up with, playing football in neighborhood backyards, chasing squirrels in the woods behind the church, building and occupying tree houses, racing bicycles, pranking one another, constantly conspiring together against parents and their somber, fun-spoiling restrictions.

Many of these same peers, now thirty-somethings like Albert, frowned at their wriggling, high-spirited children, signaling parental threats with a semaphoric combination of eyebrow raisings, piercing glances, and sternly pouted lips. In the few minutes between the time when most everyone had gathered and the liturgy actually started, Albert could see his whole life, from childhood to this moment, in a single sweep. He simply was the person all these relationships and associations had helped him become. Soon enough—the next morning, in fact—he would leave them for (at least) a while, but surveying them now and recognizing that all his life was contained in this cup called community, he thought that actually he could never go anywhere without their marks and traces on him, their spirits impressed on his spirit. And with that thought he felt a calmness and confidence locking into place, beneath the anxious uncertainty his imminent journey provoked.

He sensed Father McNearland's eyes on him and turned to face the priest. The priest smiled slightly and nodded. Then Al realized his pastor had seated him upfront not merely for the readings, but so that he would see all the people who made him what he was, and take courage.

The parish was called to order and sang the doxology. Next Father McNearland briefly framed the purpose of the service, and called Alva Simmel forward. Father McNearland vacated the pulpit and motioned for her to step behind it. Attaining the pulpit, she spread notes before her, cleared her throat, and placed flattened hands on each side of the lectern.

"You are my people," she said, "my brothers and sisters in Christ our Lord. Even though my husband has died and my son has long been on his own, I am never without family because of you. Our baptisms have made of us one family. If the Apostle Paul is to be heard, and I believe he should, the water of baptism makes us closer by common allegiance than the blood of kinship.

"Yet every family, including the church family, lives and grows by trust. I, with others who are no longer with us except by virtue of the communion of the saints, have broken that trust. You all know the details, now, and I won't rehearse them. I will tell you that I and my husband and the Harmons saw no other or better way to respond to the circumstances in which we found our children. I don't say this as an excuse. It may be that we failed in imagination, and should have seen another way. It may be that we had too little faith in you, and the aid you might have provided. Certainly we had too little faith in our children, in Valerie and Albert, who after all were dignified adults in their own right." Here she paused and turned to Al for a moment, as if in apology.

She resumed, "But whatever other possibilities there were, we concocted and enacted a deceit. We severed ourselves from this community. You *really* buried Valerie, or never doubted that you did. But we knew otherwise, and with that duplicitous knowledge we separated ourselves from you. All of you came to live in a world where Valerie was dead and lost to the living. We lived in another world, aware that she was not dead but only hidden.

"So, dear friends, I do ask for your understanding, but first I ask for your forgiveness. I ask first for your forgiveness because only it can admit my deceit and admit me back into your world, into this community, this family, of trust." She turned again to Al. "Albert, please forgive me and your father and Valerie's parents." She faced the congregation. "And all of you, please forgive me and relieve me of the secret that cut me off from you."

With that Father McNearland guided her from the pulpit and went with her to the altar rail. There he invited the whole congregation to kneel and confess its sins. When that was done the priest pronounced God's mercy and forgiveness to all. Everyone rose from their knees and Father McNearland proclaimed, "The peace of the Lord be always with you." A congregational "And also with you" resounded off the stone walls, and those nearest the stained glass windows heard them rattle. Al rushed to embrace his mother. They hugged tightly and wet each other's shoulders with their tears. Father McNearland saw fit to let the peace be celebrated in a more prolonged and raucous fashion than usual, so that for nearly a quarter hour people exchanged the peace with hugs and kisses, throughout the sanctuary. Finally the congregation quieted and folks took their seats.

Next followed a hymn, especially apropos for the occasion, Al thought. The people's voices rang out:

We are pilgrims on a journey.
We're together on the road.
We are here to help each other
Walk the mile and bear the load.

Once the song ended, the priest nodded to Al, and he rose to read the Scripture assigned for the occasion. It was from the ninth chapter of Matthew's Gospel, telling how a synagogue leader with a gravely sick daughter rushes to Jesus for help, and Jesus tardily arrives on the scene, after the girl has been given up for dead. When Al resumed his seat, Father McNearland walked to the center of the church's nave. On this occasion he was not clad in his priestly vestments, and many parishioners noticed, once again, that his legs were as bowed as a wishbone. Situated in the congregation's heart, he began.

"The Word of God often speaks for itself, and today I need add little to the text you have just heard. An anxious father comes to Jesus, desperate for his daughter's health. Jesus complies, but there are interruptions. By the time he arrives at the house of this father and his daughter, it appears too late. Mourners have gathered and are wailing in grief. Flute players have started their funeral dirges.

"We are those mourners. We have wailed in grief for one of our own daughters. We have played the songs of death at her departure. But look what happens in the Gospel story. Before Jesus even enters the house and sets eyes on the girl, he says to the noisy mourners and musicians, 'Go away; for the girl is not dead but sleeping.' The rest of Matthew's account is terse and businesslike. The mourners and other onlookers cannot believe it. Some laugh in incredulity. Jesus apparently does not argue. He simply goes inside and takes the girl by the hand, and she gets up.

"And likewise today he speaks these words to us. Valerie Harmon is not dead but—as Alva put it—has only been hidden. Christ has taken her by the hand, all along, so she stands and she walks. May she soon do so again in our midst."

What remained was for the parish to gather about Al and lay hands on him, and pray for him on his journey, then for he and Valerie on their hoped-for return. When these petitions had been made, Father McNearland collected all the prayers into his closing benediction. The blessing concluded, "Albert, on behalf of this parish and in the name of the Father, the Son, and the Holy Spirit, I send you forth. Go, and take our blessings with you. May these blessings speed you when you weary, protect you when you are in danger, and enlighten you when darkness befalls you."

"Amen," said Al with all the people. And he thought to himself: *Even if I do not know what lies before me, I know what lies behind me. Amen, amen to that.*

7

The first link in the chain leading to Valerie (presuming she was still alive and could be found—and Al stilled any thoughts otherwise) was a man called Kayak Jack. Al met him early the next morning on a dock in Old Chicago. Jack was a middle-aged man with longish graying hair and a scraggly white beard that dropped all the way to his breastbone. He wore a broad-brimmed straw hat to shade his face from the searing glare of sun on water. As his moniker suggested, his favored form of marine transportation was the kayak. He had passed two decades on the water, ferrying cargo both commercial and human across Lake Michigan. This sustained exertion resulted in a striking physique. Jack was lean, even spindly, from the waist down. But his torso and arms were broad, bulging with hard muscle. His body shape reminded Al of an upside-down pyramid, or of a tiny donkey burdened with a squat shock of hay.

Jack would lead Al to an orchard keeper on the Old Michigan side of the lake, just as he guided Valerie there five years before. The trip would take two days. Roped to Jack's kayak was another vessel on which he had securely mounted a streamlined cargo box, rectangular and narrow, and uncannily resembling a coffin. The box was the very sort that squandrels once put atop their vans or SUVs to carry heaping quantities of their stuff to vacation spots or campgrounds. (Al had read that campgrounds before the Descent were equipped with electricity, and so-called campers ran air conditioners and watched television and took hot showers. This confused him: why leave home if you wanted your camp as much like home as possible?) The cargo box rode empty and high in the water. In Old Michigan, Jack would load it with blueberries just coming into season, and fetch premium prices for the fruit on his return to Old Chicago.

Al brought along a pack with his basic travel supplies. Among other things, he was carrying a blue nylon pup tent, a sleeping bag, a fire-starter, one change of clothes, a compass and maps, a *Book of Common Prayer* and a volume of Chekov's short stories, and a .22 caliber rifle for hunting small game (rabbits, squirrels, turkeys) along the way. Al also wore a money belt with several hundred dollars in cash.

Jack and Al set out. Within minutes Al fell into a rhythm. The double-bladed paddle clipped neatly in and out of the water. With moderate and steady effort, Al's craft glided near Jack's. Al decided to trail Jack for a while and observe his technique. He watched closely to see just how deeply Jack dipped his blades beneath the surface, then worked at mimicking Jack's economical, fluid motions. Pleasurably, he found himself exerting less effort and yet moving faster. He pulled alongside Jack.

Not far off the shoreline of Old Chicago, the kayakers entered the forest of giant white windmills that provided some supply of electricity to the city. On this only slightly breezy day, the huge propellers turned lazily but, up close, still somewhat menacingly. Corpses of pigeons and ducks bobbed in the water around the towers, victims of the mills on stormier days, when the propeller blades spun faster and invisibly. Now the huge propellers rippled the water beneath them and emitted an unearthly moan, an echoing chorus of rolling, deep whooshing sounds.

Eventually Al and Jack cleared the mob of groaning towers. The kayakers stayed at their paddling, which had grown monotonous, and the towers and city skyline receded, shrinking at their backs.

The early morning sun rose like a fiery hill across the lake. The lake's creamy-smooth surface glowed hot-coal red ahead of them, while it shimmered blue and black to their sides and behind them. Al felt that thrill he always had atop deep water, the sensation that an entire, capacious world pulsed beneath him. He imagined variously sized fish sliding under him, with boulders and stringy vegetation and the occasional shipwreck looming farther below in the dark. Now and then waterfowl passed overhead, cawing raucously. Otherwise, but for Al and Jack's paddle splashes, all was still and quiet.

Jack reminisced about his earlier trip, with Valerie.

"She was a pretty thing. I thought about how beautiful she must be when she smiled. Most of the time she was with me, she was sad and mad. I could understand. I didn't know all the circumstances, but I knew she was leaving her home, leaving people behind." He looked over at Al and saw that he was listening intently.

"I tried to talk with her for a while. You could see she didn't want to talk much. She concentrated and put all her hurt and anger into the paddling. That was smart. She was smart. I let her be."

"When she got to Old Traverse, she thanked me and shook my hand. I wished her Godspeed, and she said, 'Yes. Only God knows where I'm going.' You see her again, you tell her Kayak Jack says hello." Jack tipped his hat at Al.

Then suddenly his boat flipped.

A stunned Al stared at the gleaming bottom of Jack's kayak. Al backpaddled to stay in place. Five seconds passed. Ten seconds passed . . . Al started to call out his guide's name, then the water began churning beneath the hull of Jack's craft. The churning started small, as if a washing machine's agitator boiled below, then it built to a volcanic surge. A grinning Jack burst back into the air and light.

"Hot!" he said. "And damn. That feels good." Jack shot ahead.

Al, not yet recovered from his surprise, drifted in a circle.

Jack yelled back at him, "C'mon, son. Daylight's burning."

❧

Two hours into the trip, more than daylight was burning. Al's back and arms raged in protest of this unaccustomed work. The sun had moved well above the eastern horizon and now seemed less a source of beauty than of torturing heat. Al's gloved fingers and thumbs blistered. He knew another fifteen or more hours on the water lay ahead and began to wonder how he could keep this up nearly that long. As the day warmed, Jack stopped more often for them to swig from their canteens. But he always insisted that they never remain stationary for more than a few minutes.

At noonday, they stilled their paddles and munched on beef jerky and oranges as their kayaks drifted. "Get out and take a swim," Jack said. "I'll help you back into the boat."

Al imagined the luxury of stretching his cramped legs, of moving his arms in something other than a paddling motion. It didn't take him long to slide out of the kayak and plunge beneath the cool water. He swam a broad circle around the boats, reaching as far out as he could with his arms, kicking his legs straight. He dog-paddled, then dove straight down, feeling the lake swallow his whole body. Sunlight penetrated the surface five or ten feet, and he decided to dive until he was in the dark. Once in the murk, he drew himself straight up and looked ahead into the impenetrable green. He listened to the muffled thrash of his hands and feet, to the quiet roar of his pressurized ears. He rose back into the illuminated water and, as he propelled his body in a slow rotation, saw a large pike dart across his line of sight.

It seemed only an instant after they had resumed their eastward progress before Al's back and arms ached in exactly the same places. He thought of Valerie and said silent prayers for endurance. He cussed. Then, for what seemed days instead of hours, he alternated prayers and swearing. At a couple of points in the mid-afternoon, Jack tied Al's kayak to his own. He told Al to keep paddling, to let up only a little, and part-towed Al during these intervals. At a water break, he wrapped Al's palms in gauze. The hand blisters had broken and blood leached through Al's gloves. Jack dropped the used gloves into the lake and Al put on new ones. They resumed.

Now the sun, at their rear, slowly fell westward. Al reckoned that he would never stand straight up again. He imagined that his arms would be permanently bent at the elbows. Back ashore—if he ever rested on land again—he would be a cripple, his legs forever frozen straight ahead at a ninety-degree angle from his waist, his arms and hands locked on an invisible paddle. He would move only on a board with wheels, poling himself over sidewalks and streets.

The lake stretched ahead like a vast blue desert.

He swore. He prayed.

Jack re-dressed his wounded hands and encouraged him.

Al let his exhausted but still persistent body take over. The strokes were slower and sloppier, but somehow they continued. The merciless sun dropped enough for the day to cool a little. Then Jack pointed ahead, and Al saw with him a distant vertical protuberance. It was green and tan, the green of trees, the tan of sand.

"Not long, now," Jack said. "And we're done for the day."

The island was Al's lure, a magnet that pulled him toward it, and with it in sight he found unguessed, fresh reserves of strength. Still, staring at the island made it seem ever and frustratingly distant. So Al learned to look for intervals only so far ahead as Jack's stern. Then, when he would intermittently raise his gaze, the island would be bigger and closer than it was before.

At last they slid ashore. The sand crunched and grinded under the kayaks. Al felt the forgotten sensation of solidity beneath his numb butt. Jack splashed into the shallow water, pulling all three crafts onto the beach. He pried Al's paddle from his hands and dragged him out of the kayak. Resisting the urge to kiss the dry ground, Al slowly straightened himself until he lie on his back. Then he crawled awhile. Finally he stood up and staggered off the beach, through a copse of pines, and into a clearing a hundred yards from the lakefront. Jack already had coffee percolating over a fire.

❧

Albert awoke the next morning to find himself in solitude. He looked around the campsite and sighted Jack's footprints leading away in the sand. Moving farther toward the heart of the island, he followed the footprints up and atop a dune. He looked down on a depression, out of which rose a dozen or so cedars, like toothpicks stuck higgledy-piggledy in a giant bowl of sugar. Shorn of most branches, denuded of foliage, their bark scoured away by years of blowing sand, these were known as phantom trees.

Al chased the footprints across the bowl. He topped its other side and descended into woods. The footprints disappeared, but before he could worry he saw through the trees several peculiar objects. He pressed forward and came upon rows of posts with sun-bleached bones piled around each post. Peering closely at one post, he saw markings on it, and assumed they might designate a name. He was relieved on examination to determine that the bones were animal and not human. Antlers were attached to a large skull that appeared to be part of a deer skeleton. There were smaller skulls, those of dogs and rabbits and squirrels. Rib cages of various sizes and sorts lined various piles. Leg bones protruded. A faint wind whispered through the trees and shin-high grass. Back here, where tree shade and vegetation kept the soil moist, there were still wisps of morning fog winding through the bone piles.

Al heard undergrowth and grass thrashing, and turned to face Kayak Jack.

"It's an Indian cemetery," said Jack. "They buried their dead, then surrounded them with the bones from the funeral feast. A thanksgiving, maybe. But it's a little spooky, ain't it?"

Al agreed that it was. They talked a bit more, then began their way back to camp. They collected kindling and firewood as they cleared the trees.

Just as they climbed to the top edge of dunes, Jack threw down his wood in a rush and pulled Al to his knees. "Stay low!" he said. There were binoculars strung on Jack's neck. He lifted them to his eyes, gazing out on the lake, and cursed. "Lake pirates!" He pulled the binoculars free of his neck and handed them to Al. Panning the glasses across the water, Al saw two sailboats. There were at least four men on each boat. The sails were dirty and torn. Attached to the main mast of each boat was a white flag. Al focused the binoculars. Crude skulls and crossbones adorned each of the flags, painted in the rusty brown color of what Al realized with a chill was dried blood. The pirates were perhaps a half-mile out. And they were headed directly for the spot where Jack and Al had landed the night before.

"They'll beach and see the tracks of our boats," said Jack. "Listen to me and do as I say. We don't have much time. Okay?"

Al assented.

"We could hide on the island, but the pirates will consider it fine sport to hunt us. We can't outfight them. But out here you don't survive by strength. You live by your wiles. Lake pirates are a superstitious lot, and that's our chance."

Jack instructed Al to run with him back to graveyard. There they both gathered up armfuls of the animal bones. Then they hurried back to the camp. Jack reached into the ashes of the fire and rubbed ashes on his face and through his hair, making himself look miserable and crazed. Then Jack dumped a sack of flour over Al's head. "No breakfast biscuits today," he said. Jack opened the cargo box and told Al to lie down in it. Once Al was situated, Jack scattered the bones over him.

"I'll paddle away from shore whooping and screaming, towing you behind. Stay quiet in the box until I give you the clue that we're close to the pirates. Then rock the box. And when I scream quick, three times in a row, knock the lid off and bust up out of there like dead man come back with hell's debts to collect."

Jack lowered the lid and everything went black in Al's coffin. The box jostled and slid, then Al felt it buoy up in the water. Jack was yelling as he started paddling like a madman. "Help me! Help me, God! Ghosts! Ghosts!" The cargo box rocked and tipped frightfully with Jack's manic motions. Al spread his elbows and feet against its sides in an attempt to stabilize it. Jack shouted, "Get them off of me! Get them away! Ghosts!"

Now Al detected other voices. Jack's paddle splashed wildly and Al heard flying water thump across the top of the cargo box. The towline jerked and loosened, jerked and loosened. The pirates were nearer, coarsely jeering and laughing uncertainly. They drew near enough to see Jack's begrimed face and the spittle shooting from his quivering mouth. Their laughter died when they understood it was ghosts the lunatic kayaker shouted about. Jack stopped paddling. Then Al rocked the cargo box vigorously. Water sloshed up and over it. The volume of Jack's screaming escalated. Jack started paddling again, crossing between the two sailboats.

"Yeep! Yeep! Yeep!" Jack let out.

Al pushed the lid open near the top. From each side, he stuck out a blistered hand, wrapped in blood-crusted, unwinding gauze and tape. The pirates went silent.

Al popped the box lid off and sat up. Skulls of various shapes and sizes flew into the air and chunked against the hulls of the sailboats. Al's kicking feet shot deer femurs and rabbit legs high over the water. A squirrel paw stuck out from between Al's lips and antlers hung off one shoulder. There he sat, white as death.

Al released the most fearsome, bloodcurdling scream he could muster. Then the pirates exploded with their own screams, to a man. They commenced a furious flurry. On one boat, pirates stuck long oars over the side and dug water to speed their departure from Kayak Jack and his pursuing ghost. On the other, they swung sail into the wind and heeled away, sending one pirate overboard. The dismounted buccaneer swam in a panic after his boat, grabbed at the line thrown to him and was jerked away, screaming and gurgling in the boat's wake.

In a minute the pirate crafts were moving out of earshot, away from the island and its haunts, back out into the relative safety of the lake's open waves.

The rocking of Al's and Jack's vessels slowed. The water foamed around them. Al spat bits of gobby flour out of his mouth and picked tiny bones out of his hair. Jack grinned.

"Hot," he said. "And damn!"

8

From the island to the Old Michigan shoreline was another thirty miles, so Al found himself landed on the docks of Old Traverse Bay late in the afternoon following the encounter with the lake pirates. Al and Jack said their goodbyes, then Al gathered his pack of supplies and proceeded into a dockside supply store. Here, he figured, was as good a place as any to ask after the orchard keeper, one Lea Hanson, into whose hands Valerie had been entrusted five years before.

The small store appeared well stocked with foodstuffs. But it also carried an unpredictable mélange of other goods. Against a near wall leaned post hole diggers, a couple of used and weathered axes, a pair of snowshoes with taped repairs, and an ancient Victrola phonograph player. There was no one behind the counter, near the cash register, but Albert could hear voices in the back of the store. He wound through a maze of shelves and found the apparent proprietor in conversation with a man who gazed up at a framed painting. Al peeked—it was Warner Sallman's famous twentieth-century portrait of a burnished, glowing Jesus.

The customer's jeans were muddy, his face unwashed, his hatband coated with greasy dirt. The obviously well-traveled man aimed a gnarly finger at the painting. "Now, who is that? Wild Bill Hickok?"

"No," said the storekeeper, a middle-aged woman wearing an apron and an accountant's green visor. "Jesus Christ!"

"Well," the customer jerked his finger down and reared back, "no need to get temperamental and cuss about it. I'm just asking."

The storekeeper chuckled. "I'm not cussing about it. The man in the painting is supposed to be Jesus Christ." With that the traveler had a laugh at himself, and went ahead to wander the aisles of the rest of the store.

Al stepped forward, under the pensive profile of Christ, and the storekeeper asked what she could do for him.

"Ma'am, I'm looking for Lea Hanson. I understand she has an orchard around here."

"Mama Lea?" the storekeeper said. "I knew her well. She's dead now, been gone three years or more. But I can tell you where her orchard is."

Al was stunned. Lea Hanson was the contact Kayak Jack had given him, the would-be informant who would point him to the next stop in the trail that would eventually lead to Valerie. His stomach climbed up his spine—if he couldn't talk to Lea Hanson, how would he know where to go next? But he recovered his composure and said he would like directions to what once was the Hanson orchard.

Al stumbled back out into the sunlight. He wondered if Jack had been unaware of Mama Lea's death, or had known and simply didn't want to admit the bad news to Al. He looked back down by the docks and saw that Jack and his kayaks had disappeared. He decided to visit the orchard—maybe the present keeper would know the secret of Valerie's next stop, or know who Al might talk to in order to gain the secret. He hiked inland, following the storekeeper's directions.

After an hour's walk, Albert was near the end of a finger of land laid in the bay. He saw the easy rolling hills and lined grapevines of an orchard. The air was sweet, the sunlight soft on his shoulders, but Al couldn't quell his anxiety. Had Valerie's trail gone cold so soon? How bitter it would be if he had to give up his journey after it had barely started, to return alone to his home and church less than a week after he had departed.

At this juncture he came even with one long row of vines and saw a man in overalls about halfway down it. The man was pulling out dried tendrils and otherwise fussing at the vines. Al waved at him and, when the wave was returned, climbed through a wooden railed fence into the vineyard.

He gave the worker his name.

"Hello. And my name is Jeremy Wiltner," the worker answered in an entirely friendly and open manner.

"I've come from Old Chicago," Al said. "I hoped to visit Lea Hanson, but I'm told she's gone."

"Ah, dear Mama Lea. Yes, she's no longer with us."

"So you knew, uh, Mama Lea?"

"I did. Very well, for many years."

Al considered what to ask next. "Mr. Wiltner, did she ever mention a Valerie Harmon to you?"

"Valerie Harmon . . . It rings no bells, I'm afraid."

"Well," Al said as his hopes plunged, "were there others that knew Mama Lea better than you? Family or such?"

For the first time Wiltner looked wary. But he elected to remain friendly. "There is a son, Peter Hanson. I don't want to speak ill of anybody, but Peter is a bit of a wastrel—some would say he's flat-out no good. After Mama Hanson died he kept this orchard for a year or two. I should say he was *supposed* to keep it. He drank away his days and nights. Those of us who work vineyards would say he paid too much attention to wine in the bottle and forgot all about the wine on the vine. This place was a disgraceful mess, and finally Peter sold it to me."

"I see," said Al.

"It's taken two years to get it back into some kind of shape." He swatted at a dangling, shriveled and rotten grape. "And it still needs plenty of work."

Al considered again. "I suppose I need to talk to Peter Hanson." He grasped at the possibility that the son, however laggardly and wayward, might still have possessed some shreds of his mother's trust, and been left with the vital information of Valerie's itinerary.

"Good luck with finding Peter," Wiltner said. "This was Peter's home. It was a splendid vineyard, and it will be again, mark my word. But he gave it up. He gave himself up. I have no idea where his home is now, if the poor sot has a home."

Al took that in, felt despair gathering in him like an avalanche on the verge of breaking. Then, all at once, another possible inquiry occurred to him. He remembered that the Romans 16 network had a passcode. And perhaps Jeremy Wiltner was a part of the network and knew something about Valerie. And perhaps he was being careful not to divulge it to any old stranger passing by. Of course! He should have started with the passcode in the first place. His spirits rose and bucked with fresh possibility.

He spouted out the first half of the code: "Praise God who strengthens us according to the gospel and proclamation of Jesus."

His hopes crashed as quickly as Wiltner absorbed this sudden declaration. The orchard keeper's smile vanished and a shield fell over his countenance. "Now look here, are you a Jehovah's Witness or some kind of religious fanatic? I've got work to do. Why don't you high-step it off my property and let me get back to it."

Al apologized and fled.

By the time he had hiked back into town it was dinnertime. The avalanche of despair broke and bore down on Al. He was thirsty, though he had no appetite. He found a bar, where he ate little and drank a lot. Darkness was falling, so he entered a hotel and bought a room. He kicked off his shoes and lay down without peeling the blankets of the bed back. He started to pray. A serious case of the hiccups commenced. He decided the hiccups was all the prayer he had in him, and slept fitfully.

❧

Morning brought with it the headache and dry mouth of a hangover. Al washed and headed out for some breakfast. Not far from the hotel was a restaurant. As Al approached, the door swung open and a man roughly dragged through it a skinny, worn-out woman. "Get out and stay out," the man barked. "My customers don't need you around here begging and ruining their meal."

The woman collapsed onto the steps of the stoop outside the restaurant's door. Her nose and cheekbones and limbs were craggy and sharp-angled. All her smoothness was rubbed away, her lissome curves of body and spirit abraded by suffering. Her short-sleeved arms bore ugly purple and yellow bruises. Most alarmingly, there was a scabby, long cut down one side of her face. For a moment Al forgot his own misery. He sat down beside her.

"What were you trying to get to eat in there?" he asked her.

"I just want a little something to eat. And that bastard threw me out."

"I'm going in for something to eat," Al said. "And if you'll tell me what you'd like, I'll get it with my breakfast and come back out to eat with you."

The woman registered surprise, and for the first time looked directly in his eyes. "Would you really, mister?"

"I would."

"Okay, then," she paused, still in amazement. "I'd like a biscuit sandwich, a biscuit with cheese and ham on it."

Al went inside and ordered two ham-and-cheese biscuit sandwiches to go, plus a couple of cups of coffee. Once the waitress delivered the food and drink in a grease-spotted paper bag, Al paid and returned to the haggard woman.

She thanked him profusely. For a while the pair ate in silence, nibbling at the biscuits and sipping the steaming coffee. Then Al offered his name, and the woman replied that her name was Lisa.

"Looks like you've been hurt," Al said.

"It was a bicycle accident," Lisa replied. But she hardly tried to disguise the lie. She said it rotely, automatically, like a line that had been rehearsed but could not be delivered with any conviction.

"A bicycle accident?" Al said skeptically.

With that she tried to muster more sincerity. "Yeah. You know, fell off my bike on my face."

Then she changed the subject. They discussed the weather and agreed on its magnificence. They talked about how fine the biscuits tasted, how the ham had been grilled to just the right crispness and juiciness. By then Al was thinking again about his day, his troubles, feeling his urgency about locating Peter Hanson. When Lisa sensed he was ready to go, she ardently thanked him again for the meal.

He stood up. "You're welcome. It's good to meet you, Lisa. And, if there is a God, God bless you."

He couldn't have told exactly why he'd said the last, offering the half-hearted blessing. Part of it was because he felt bereft and doubtful. Another part of it was the woman's condition, and his intuitive guess that God talk would very easily ring hollow to someone in her straits. But she reacted with shock, with a degree of surprise greater than her own earlier surprise that a stranger was offering her a meal.

"Look, I really appreciate the food. But I have to say, Al, I don't know how I would make it another day if I didn't believe there is a God."

It was Al's turn to be surprised. He had thought he was doing her a favor, being sensitive to her circumstances, in addressing her without any hint of piety. But that was not how she had taken his remark. She thanked him again for the food, but was now clearly in a hurry to go on her way. Al watched her depart. Then he went back into the restaurant, to begin queries about the whereabouts of Peter Hanson.

❧

Al spent the rest of day walking the streets of Old Traverse, ducking in and out of shops, restaurants, hotels, and other establishments, at every stop inquiring after Hanson and coming out empty handed. A few folk knew of the Hanson family, and had known Peter, but were unaware of his current location. In these post-Descent decades, few telephone services worked reliably outside metropolitan areas, so Al found what he expected when he consulted the negligibly thin Old Traverse phone book—no listing of Peter Hanson. He thought of visiting the police, but subs never knew what sort of uninvited attention they might elicit if they involved themselves with the authorities. The cops would surely ask their own questions. If he said anything about the National Anti-Natal Law's repeal and his hunt for his lover, they might interpret what he said as a criticism of the Constituency, and no such criticisms were suffered lightly. And if he said little in answer to their inevitable questions, they might grow suspicious and jail him as a vagrant or even a possible terrorist.

The fruitless hours of wandering did little to ease Al's growing sense of panic. To avert dwelling on his anxiety, he directed his thoughts to the encounter with the poor woman that morning.

On the one hand, someone might say Lisa's unwavering faith was a blind trust born of desperation. She was hungry, living from one meal to another, perhaps homeless and certainly impoverished. She was probably in an abusive relationship—he didn't for a second believe those bruises and cuts were the result of a bicycle accident, or any other kind of accident. So the woman was living a hard life. What was that twentieth-century phrase he'd heard, that there are no atheists in foxholes? In her sorry circumstances, she had little to cling to other than the hope that there was a loving, ultimately concerned God.

But on the other hand, Al now recognized how easy it had been for him to toss out his doubting words. He was by no means rich, and decidedly a subordinate, but he had a comfortable home, he had considerable education, he had supportive family and friends, he had enough money to light out on a road trip. Maybe his doubt was a kind of luxury Lisa could never afford. With a never starved stomach and fairly secure life, maybe he played at agnosticism, dabbled like a dilettante or a hypocricket in atheism. He was reminded of Tolstoy's comment that the relatively well off can embrace "a faith that is not really faith but only one of the epicurean consolations in life," a hobby alongside other indulgences that distracts us from the reality of our impending deaths. It took little courage to climb on to the high wire of skepticism while knowing there were strong nets to catch you if you fell. Lisa's faith was something different. There was nothing to catch her if it failed. To her it was in no degree a game. It was sheerly a matter of life and death. He reconsidered all of his casual assumptions about the beggars he had regularly passed on the streets of Old Chicago. He had tried to be compassionate on those occasions, to offer some change and a smile. But he had always on some level considered the beggars pitiable, as weak and beaten people. Now he saw them in another light. The beggars, at least those like Lisa, were spiritual masters, brave, persevering giants of faith who graciously tolerated the condescension of the deluded spiritual dwarves who daily passed them by with invincible ignorance and smugness.

❧

At evening's arrival, Al looped back toward the hotel. He wished not to spend another night there, or tarrying anywhere in Old Traverse, but he seemed to have no choice. With no gleanings of Peter Hanson or another lifeline to Mama Hanson's secret, he would have to resume his search tomorrow. Perhaps he would visit churches and soup kitchens, asking and searching for the broken trail of breadcrumbs that would take him to Valerie. Tonight he would pray for determination, and maybe for a little luck.

At that moment he heard a greeting from behind him.

"Hello, Al."

He turned and saw that it was Lisa.

"I've seen you tramping up and down these streets all day. This morning you asked me some questions. Now it's my turn. What are you doing here, Al?"

He was glad to see her, the closest thing to a friend he had in this town.

"Hello to you, Lisa, and nice to see you again. I'm looking for someone."

"You're looking for someone? Who are you looking for?"

He could imagine no harm in giving her the name. He had asked it of two dozen other people that day.

"I'm looking for a man named Peter Hanson."

Her jaw went slack, her eyes opened wide. "I didn't give you my name, not my full name. My name is Lisa Hanson. Peter Hanson is my husband."

"What?" he startled back at her. Then he checked a mounting joy with wariness. Was her Peter the same man he was searching for, or just someone with the same name? "Is your husband the son of Lea Hanson?"

She smiled broadly, unguardedly. "He is one and the same. See, you should have asked me in the first place."

Exactly right. Peter had assumed the battered and hungry woman could only receive help, and had nothing to give. His assumptions about beggars, about giving and receiving—it seemed so many of them were misguided.

"What do you want from Peter Hanson?" Lisa asked.

"I just need to ask him a few questions. He may have some information his mother left for me."

"All right, then. Let me introduce you to Peter Hanson."

She led him away from the center of town. In half an hour they were entering dilapidated suburbs. They made small talk, Al telling her what sort of work he was in, where he was from; Lisa describing the last job she'd held, harvesting beans and melons, how she had grown up in Old Ohio and moved to Old Michigan looking for work, after she was orphaned in high school.

Soon it was apparent they were drawing near to the Hanson home. Lisa began to greet by name people they passed on the street. They came upon a neighborhood of small ranch houses, all in greater or lesser degree of disrepair. Roofs needed shingles replaced, siding had scalped off walls in patches, paint had worn away to expose gray wood underneath. Several houses fronted the street with gutters that had gone uncleaned for years, so that tall weeds and even tree saplings had grown up out of them.

Lisa slowed her pace. She appeared nervous.

"There," she said, "that little yellow house. Peter's in there, sleeping off a drunk. I don't want to see him right now."

Albert paused.

"Go on," she said with a wave toward the house. "Let yourself in." And as he crossed the lawn to the front door, she retreated back down the street.

He knocked on the door several times. Then he spoke loudly, "Peter, Peter Hanson! Can I come in?"

There was no answer from inside. He tried the doorknob and it turned. He pushed the door open slightly and called again. Still no answer. He stepped into the house. The room was dark, all curtains closed to what feeble light remained to the day. A redheaded man in a T-shirt stumbled into the room, zipping and belting his jeans as he advanced.

"Whaddya want? What the hell is it?" Peter Hanson said, and then he saw that his visitor was a stranger.

"Who are you? What are you doing in my house?"

Al raised a hand. "Hold on. Please. I was told I might find you here. And I just want to ask you a question."

Hanson stopped. "What kind of question?"

"You may have information for me. Something maybe your mother told you."

Hanson grimaced in confusion. Al cut to the chase: "If you know what I'm asking for, this will mean something to you. 'Praise God who strengthens us according to the gospel and proclamation of Jesus.'"

Hanson livened, seemed to emerge from a haze. He sat down on a worn couch. "When Mama was dying, she told me over and over again that someone might come with those words. She made me repeat the response back to her: 'According to the revelation of the mystery that was kept secret for long ages.'"

Just like that, tears welled in Al's eyes. He sat on the far end of the couch. Peter Hanson told him he needed to proceed to a small town in southern Old Michigan, a town called Old Latimer. There he was to visit the sole Pentecostal church in the town, housed in the former First Presbyterian building. The church gardener would know and tell Al what he needed to know next.

"I don't know what to say," Al said in the quiet. "Thank you. Thank you very much."

Hanson rubbed his beard. "I was a punk, maybe sixteen or seventeen, when they brought that girl to my house. She seemed like something special. I hope you find her."

Al thanked him again. Then he decided to say more.

"Peter, I don't know you. I don't know what's happened in your life. It seems like you're having a hard time. But I'm asking you—no, I'm telling you—don't take it out on Lisa."

Hanson flinched and anger rose in his eyes.

"Listen," said Al. "She didn't tell me anything about what you might do to her. There's no blame on her part. All I'm saying is, you hope I find my girl, the woman I love like life itself. And I hope you don't lose your girl."

Hanson relaxed a bit, and Al went on. "You may have lost your sense of purpose, a reason for living. But I'm telling you, you have a purpose. I know you do, because you were here when I came looking, and you have told me what I need to know."

There was silence, but Peter was looking at him, expectantly.

Al dared to add, "Your mother's faith—in God, in you—it wasn't for nothing."

He left the house and resumed the street. At the first large thoroughfare he turned the corner and had to stop himself from running. He felt like he could never be tired again. He didn't know how far he would go that night, but he knew he would go south, and however far he went, he would be that much closer to Valerie. In the distance ahead of him, clouds built into towering banks, and lightning played in and behind them like great hearths burning from inside a fortress. A pillar of fire and smoke went before him, and led him on.

9

The next few weeks passed uneventfully, and for this Albert was thankful. He arrived in Latimer and readily located the Presbyterian become Pentecostal church. He came upon the church gardener picking juicy, thick green worms off rows of tomato plants. After some small talk, he recited the first half of the Romans 16 passcode, and immediately received in reply the affirmative second half of the code. He successfully repeated this procedure on two more occasions, in two other towns, and kept moving steadily closer to Valerie.

His days lulled into a reassuring, if not entirely comfortable, routine. He rose with the sun, started a fire, then warmed meat left over from the previous day's hunt, scrambled eggs if he had recently been lucky enough to raid a pheasant's nest, and toasted bread. He washed down the food with hot coffee. He luxuriated in a second cup of scalding coffee, and over it sent up his morning prayers, imagining them wafting heavenward with the steam lofting from his cup. Then he packed and lit out. He walked mile after mile. He followed maps and the fragmented remains of state and Interstate highways toward his next destination. He watched the sky rolling by, sedately blue and white, with delicately floating marzipan clouds—until it would, on some days, steadily give way to dark turbulence, and the rushing clouds would turn into dirty gray clots of cotton. He tried to anticipate inclement weather, and take shelter in abandoned barns or beneath the massive concrete bulk of bridges stretching across the crumbled Interstates. Every day, he consumed an ambulatory lunch, munching on beef jerky and crackers and cheese and fruit as he walked. He kept his canteen full and his heart, as much as he could, empty.

The empty heart was preferable in that once he began thinking of Val (and his possible child—my God, he was probably already a father!) his thoughts might stumble like a hapless drunk into a muddy ditch of doubt and apprehension. Perhaps Valerie was no longer alive. Maybe she never made it to a place of security and respite, those years that now seemed a lifetime ago. And if she was alive, maybe she had met someone and gotten married in the period since Al and she were parted. Or even if she hadn't "met someone," maybe she had acclimated to the single life and done her best to forget about Al, and maybe she wouldn't really want her détente with time and circumstance interrupted or altered . . .

In all events, however vertiginously the cliffs fell open and gaping in the topography of his inner life, Al kept one foot successively marching forward in front of the other. He stopped for the day only when night or weather necessitated stopping. He built a sandwich and a fire. He gazed meditatively at the moon, hanging above him like a globular piece of white driftwood. He slept under the stars or in his tent or in a forgotten house, awakening often to bird or animal sounds in the night, then, the sounds folding into his dreams, drifting back to sleep. Eventually he stirred with the dawn, and started another day over again.

It was not a bad life. He had a point and a destination (however uncertain its results), and every day he could account for literal progress. He was intermittently lonely, but then loneliness had haunted him even back home, in the city, when he was often surrounded by people. And there were times—most certainly, there were times—when euphoria and something more solid, something like hope, enveloped him and buoyed his spirit. And at such times he was sure Val awaited him, wanted him and longed for him. Then his mind filled with pictures of her delicious hips as she climbed stairs in front of him, or of her simply smiling on him or taking his hand without thought or hesitation. Could life ever, or need it ever, get much better than an open road traversed in the company of dreams?

❧

Al reckoned he was in the southern tip of Old Indiana when he sauntered into a town called Piedmont, and marked a sign signaling a population of two thousand. It was noonish, and he planned to treat himself to a sit-down restaurant lunch. He was still on the outskirts of town when he heard the low, angry growl of a dog. He glanced to his right and saw a pit bull, one leg hiked high, darkening a spot on the otherwise gray and weathered wood of a rickety outhouse.

Al sped his pace at the menacing sound, but the dog raced into the street. It suddenly stopped just inches from where he stood. It crouched on all four legs and reared back, then it sprang. In a split second that seemed an eternity he saw the flying beast's mottled brown and black coloring, its muscled chest, the ribbon of saliva sluicing out from between sharp, jagged teeth. Instinctually, Al tore the pack from his back and swung it round, striking his attacker on its shoulders. The dog, with paws churning, rolled in mid-air and landed on its back. Adrenalinized, ratcheted into a sheer, primitive state of survival, Al stepped toward the dog and kicked it, hard, right in the head. The dog yelped in pain. Then—

"Godfrey!" a man shouted sternly. Emerged from the outhouse was a middle-aged man with an elaborate handlebar mustache. He wore trousers tucked into the uppers of his black boots, and a frock coat with four red bandannas tied around his right arm. The dog whimpered, stood and shook as if dispelling the daze from the head blow, then sheepishly hobbled off and sat at its master's side.

"You, sir, why are you molesting my dog?" The man spoke with an air of assumed authority, with a confidence born of long and unquestioned entitlement.

"What? No, wait . . ." Al started.

"Godfrey, are you all right?" The man bent to inspect the dog, rubbing its ears, patting each eye, prying its mouth open. The dog growled quietly, in muted protest of the brisk examination.

Al found his voice. "I did not 'molest' your dog. I'm just passing through, and it attacked me."

"The animal's name is Godfrey, sir, and you may so address him. As for an attack on your person: nonsense! Godfrey's training disallows unprovoked attacks." The man snapped into an erect, soldierly posture, as if to prove the dog's customary military environment.

Two or three other people had appeared in the midst of the excitement. Now one of them, a wiry little man with two red bandannas wrapped around his arm, spoke. "You don't know who you're quibbling with, stranger. This"—and he faced the dog master and bolted to attention—"is General Aloysius Spartacus Piedmont, supreme commander of the Piedmont County platoons. And mayor of our fair town."

"Harrumph," the general cleared his throat in affirmation and demonstration of his nobility.

Al had heard of private armies scattered across parts of rural Old America. It had apparently been his misfortune to stumble into the hands of one such outfit.

"Should we arrest this man, sir?" barked the little man.

The general extracted gauntleted leather gloves from the pocket of his coat, and slid his hands into them ceremoniously, as if they would fit him for the demanding moral and mental labor he must now undertake.

"Violence against an innocent animal—and that animal our dear Godfrey! The mascot of our fighting forces, the totem of our prowess and courage, the hound of horror haunting all our enemies! This brutish behavior cannot pass without serious redress." The general turned his glare directly on Al. "You, sir, are now faced with a choice. You may either submit to a public lashing and leave our town immediately following your humiliation."

"Ten-hut!" the toady unaccountably cried, and now the half-dozen men gathered about the general clicked their boot heels and jerked ramrod straight.

"Or," the general resumed. "Or, you may join the Piedmont County Army and serve in it, under me—and with uninterrupted respect to our dear Godfrey—for a term of one full year."

Al was incredulous. As more men—apparently soldiers—drifted to Piedmont's side, Al abandoned the idea of making a break for it. He would be quickly apprehended. The public lashing (barbaric!) would get him out of town soonest, but at what cost to his body and spirit? He decided that he would enlist in the private army. Here stood its supreme commander with his ridiculous demeanor, himself and his forces marking their rank with red bandannas flapping on their arms. Such a ramshackle outfit ought to be one he could escape easily enough, and soon enough. He would join the army, ostensibly, and in a few days slip off and away, back to his travels.

"Well, what say you?" General Piedmont demanded.

"I say I will join your army. Uh, sir. With all due respect to you and Godfrey, sir."

"Very well, then. We shall test your mettle with training starting tomorrow." The general pointed at a black, potbellied man with one red bandanna wrapped just below his shoulder. "You, there, Corporal Hallenbacher. Escort our new recruit to his barracks."

"And you, soldier," General Piedmont again addressed Al. "What is your name?"

"Al Simmel, sir."

"Very well, then." The general grimaced. "Damned if this excitement hasn't aggravated my kidneys." He marched back into the outhouse and slammed the door shut behind him. Godfrey gave Al one last guttural burst of disapproval for good measure, then trotted beside the outhouse and hiked a leg to paint another spot behind his undried earlier application.

❧

The corporal situated Al in the barracks—what looked most certainly to be an old chicken coop—and left Al to wait while he fetched sheets and a pillow for the bunk bed on which the novice soldier would slumber. Once returned, the corporal glanced about, made sure the two were alone, then broke into a wide smile.

"This is some crazy carnival, huh?"

Al was surprised at an officer's casual attitude toward his army, and unsure how to respond. "It's kind of wild, corporal."

"Ah, don't 'corporal' me." He punched Al on the shoulder lightly. "My real name is Dusty Longsinger. Call me Dusty unless we're in earshot of the general."

Dusty Longsinger then explained that he had been in the Piedmont County Army for two years. He was wandering through town when the general mistook him for a comrade in arms from an earlier military campaign. The general wined and dined Dusty—whom he reminisced with as "old Hallenbacher"—for four days and nights, and then offered him immediate officer status as a Piedmont County regular. By then Dusty had remembered how comfortable sedentary, non-nomadic existence could be, so he took up the general's offer.

"I've gotten used to it. It's a pretty easy life, with only the occasional battle. And those usually don't take long and don't get too nasty. I mean, there's not a lot to fight over around here. Every few years some upstart town will try to claim the county seat, and we skirmish and keep the seat here in Piedmont. Once all the barbers in this and two adjoining counties tried to put together a cartel, and charge exorbitant rates for their services. We routed their little ragtag fighting force in one afternoon, and got free haircuts that night."

Dusty found life in the Piedmont Army vastly entertaining. "You can't make this stuff up," he said. "And it's almost as diverting as a fifty dollar striptease." He recounted how the general was given to flights of inadvertently hilarious oratory invoking ancestral sacrifices, especially before or immediately after battle.

"So, before one battle, we mustered in this corral outside a huge barn. This was the site of a war some years before to secure fertilizer for the general's expansive cropland. All the 'product,' shall we say, of thirty horses and forty milk cows was shoveled into a small mountain in the corner of the corral. General Piedmont was determined to inspire us. He drew his long sword and climbed to the top of the pile. Up there he struck a pose and shouted down at us, 'Men, soldiers who came before you fought and died for this shit!'"

Dusty shook with laughter. This anecdote reminded him of another, and similar, occasion. The general strived mightily to incite passion for a crusade to keep cockfighting legal in Piedmont County. Addressing his troops with more and more fervency, he finally lifted two fists to the sky and declared, "Men! We must fight with valor and undaunted determination! Our forefathers founded this county with their Bibles in one hand and their cocks in the other!"

Once Dusty finished wheezing with laughter, he said again that better entertainment was not to be found anywhere or anyhow. "So stick around, son, and you'll have some stories to tell." Abruptly, his smile vanished, his visage assumed a dreadful sobriety. "And you do *not* want to mess with that whipping."

Al decided he liked Dusty Longsinger. But he hoped not to stick around too long.

Then a question occurred to Al, so long as Longsinger was ready to talk about their commander in chief.

"What's with the dog pissing every time the general does?"

Dusty's levity returned in an instant. "A medical marvel, ain't it? Hardly know what to make of it. But the army doc says General Piedmont and Godfrey have 'sympathetic bladders.'"

With that he was lost in another fit of appreciative laughter, like a gourmet savoring the range and piquancy of spices enjoyed at every meal, past and future.

10

Al lay awake in the barracks. His bunkmates snored. Moonlight washed in a window and illuminated a wall clock. 3:30 a.m. The unfamiliar surroundings prevented Al from drifting into the sweet oblivion of sleep.

Al was forced into soldier training over several days. Drilling and training with his fellow soldiers usually wore him out so that slumber came effortlessly. But during today's exercises the general had pontificated at length about valor and physical courage. The talk reminded him of Valerie's courage and resourcefulness. Her family told innumerable stories about her rescuing frightened cousins from treetops, leaping off a swimming pool's high dive when children twice her age still shied from the top board, standing down and evacuating an angry badger that wandered into the backyard.

The episode Al remembered most included him. On a midwinter's day Valerie appeared at his doorstep. A neighbor's child was feverish and perhaps veering into a potentially lethal pneumonia. Val asked Al to walk with her the mile to the nearest doctor, to attain medicine for the little boy. Of course Al agreed. Feathery snow began falling before they reached the physician's home. The day was already blustery, and as the storm rolled in the wind picked up. By the time they arrived and secured the medicine, a full blizzard was in force. Visibility was two feet, three at the most. It appeared that the boy's would-be rescuers would have to wait out the blizzard in the shelter of the doctor's house.

But Valerie would hear nothing of it. The blizzard might last hours, even through the night, and the boy needed the medicine immediately. Val paced and thought, staring out the white-blanked windows. Then she smiled and presented her solution. She asked the doctor if she and Al could borrow two ropes. The doctor rummaged in his basement and came up with two thirty-feet-long lariats.

Val's idea was that she and Al would secure one rope apiece around their waists, then advance by following the ropes in relay. As one forged ahead to the next tree or fence or street sign, the other would remain stationary at the just-attained landmark. Tied to the stationary partner, the venturing partner could safely grope his or her way to next station. Like mountain climbers, except moving horizontally rather than vertically, they would repeat the maneuver all the way back to the neighbor's house.

Al recalled the crushing whiteness, enveloping them like a bright, cramped tunnel. He recalled an odd sort of claustrophobia, one that prodded panic even as he stumbled through openness. He remembered how the rope would tauten, then he would arc back and forth at the rope's extremity until he kicked or touched or just banged his nose into a landmark. At that point he would jerk the rope three times in quick succession, and Val would advance from behind to his side. After two, maybe three hours they achieved the mailbox of a neighbor just three doors' down from the ailing boy's home. They paused there, and laughed in anticipation of their near triumph. They hugged and Val rose on her tiptoes and Al kissed her, gently, on her mouth.

The medicine was delivered. The storm did not abate until well into the next day, and by then the serum had broken the fever. When it was definite that the boy was recovering, his parents poured scotch and toasted Valerie and Albert. Al looked into Val's green eyes and said, "You know, you really are something. You are an incredible person." She chuckled and pretended the rescue was entirely his idea.

Awake in the pale moonlight, the barracks clock now advanced to four, Al prayed silently. "A woman that brave, Lord, a woman that plucky and resourceful, surely she has survived. God, you watched over her and me in that snowstorm. Watch over us now, help me to grope and stumble through to her." Then, at last, he dozed.

❧

For the Piedmont County Regulars, the day began at 6:30, with a trumpeter blowing reveille. The forty-three soldiers came into the daylight, cussing and grumbling about their interrupted slumber. They fell into ranks and went quiet when a lieutenant appeared. He called them to order and marched them to breakfast.

From eight until noon, they engaged in a variety of training exercises. As a new recruit, Al had not been assigned his permanent role in the fighting forces. So, with Dusty Longsinger leading him, he went from place to place and a variety of training duties. Eventually the general himself would assign Al to the infantry, cavalry, navy, or air force, according to his aptitude as revealed in training.

Infantry of course involved men who would charge on foot into the enemy's maw. The infantry troops carried rifles, former hunting equipment requisitioned from the homes of Piedmont County taxpayers. Training then consisted of acquaintance with firearms and a good deal of shooting practice. Since infantry would be engaged in hand-to-hand combat, there was also training with knives and clubs. In terms of heavy artillery, the infantry possessed a catapult, two large and mounted crossbows from which were fired flaming harpoons, and a generous supply of fireworks that had been "donated" by a traveling vendor who did not want either to take a lashing or serve a term in Piedmont's army.

Al possessed excellent eyesight and proved an able and accurate rifleman. The knife- and club-fighting suited him less, since he was thin and light. But he was agile, and with training would not be casually bested. Shooting the harpoons required minimal skill, since accuracy here entailed, literally, being able to hit the side of a barn, and set it (or a haystack or a dry pasture) ablaze. Ditto with the fireworks, which were laid in a forked mount and ignited at a thirty-degree angle from the ground—thus their loads could be fired at earthbound objects, rather than at the sky.

Al met with less success at the surprisingly arcane art of catapulting. The catapults were small, their levering beam measuring out to fifteen feet. In his eagerness to please his instructor, Al hurried from the rock pile, slung, and fired one of the weapons before it had been properly aimed. The small boulder shot through the roof of the mess hall, then smashed the only waffle grill owned by the army. This meant not only an airy, drafty mess hall until the roof was repaired, but the cessation of breakfast waffles—a favorite staple for many of the troops. For his precipitous efforts Al earned a season of unpopularity and a nickname: the Waffle Killer.

The Waffle Killer showed more promise as a potential cavalryman. Since his postman-father had kept horses, Al was an experienced rider. With his experience and his light weight, Al had to hold back his mount to prevent racing ahead of the rest of charging cavalry. He was surprised that three members of the cavalry were terrible riders, but soon learned why. These recruits showed up drunk—or grossly hung over—on the day of a battle. For punishment, they were tied into their saddles—facing backward—and were frightfully carried helter-skelter, into and out of lines of fire, by their confused and spooked mounts. They would remain cavalrymen for a term, even though they hardly steered their horses better facing the front than from the rear. But the stunt, however effectively it served as discipline, lowered the entire cavalry's morale. Since the unit consisted of ten to twelve soldiers, a quarter or more of its troops were terminally inept on horseback and constantly complaining about their sore asses. Al hoped not to be assigned to the cavalry.

Navy training came next. Naval duty was objectionable to most of the soldiers. The navy's three gunboats were of use only if an enemy would engage on water. And both of landlocked Piedmont County's lakes lay nowhere near a border with another county. Thus the lakes were of little strategic importance. Once in awhile a scuffle might occur near the banks of a river, but the gunboats were too large for river deployment. This the navy had learned to its embarrassment in a recent engagement. A gunboat had sailed off the lake and down a river. But a few hundred yards short of the fray, it ran aground. This left the soldiers in position as sitting ducks and ship was abandoned. It turned out that one of sailors could not swim. He had flailed and screamed alongside the boat, his head bobbing in and out of the water. Finally someone convinced him to stand up and when he did so the water level rose only to his thighs. He commenced sheepishly ashore.

Needless to say, it was Dusty Longsinger, with his acute eye for folly and foibles, who regaled Al with the various histories of the army's misadventures. Mostly, Dusty averred, Piedmont's army, like those of his various enemies, consisted of grown men who wanted to play with explosives and other diverting toys. They didn't truly want to maim or kill other men, so most gunshots threatened treed squirrels and birds more than the enemy soldiers. Big booms that spectacularly destroyed old and empty buildings were also favored. Dusty had done quite a bit of reading on military history, and he said the armies of history had to work hard at convincing and training soldiers to kill other men. It was surprising, for instance, that many of the muskets collected from Civil War battlefields still contained their charges, meaning that they were never fired even as men charged the lines of the opposition. Dusty also observed that picnickers lounged for spectators' sport beside some of the first battlefields of the American Civil War. And almost always nations had gone into wars thinking and claiming each war would be short and easily won. Typically, one US official in the early twenty-first century boasted that an invasion of a country then called Iraq would be "a cakewalk." Of course, most wars turned out to be bloodier and longer than anticipated. But it seemed that hard-won knowledge was quickly forgotten, in plenty of time before the next conflict. "What it all adds up to," Dusty reckoned, "is that people like the idea of war more than war itself, but they like that *idea* an awful lot."

In all events, Al had one more Piedmont County military specialty to try. That was the air force, which owned nine one-man dirigibles. Each Kevlar-coated dirigible was ten feet long, and had mounted to its bottom a pedal apparatus connected to a propeller at the balloon's end. A well-conditioned man (or woman—there were two women in the air force) could pedal and propel a dirigible at an impressive clip. The crafts were also fitted with steam-thrusters, which would speed a dirigible to fifteen or twenty miles an hour. This would work only at short intervals, however, since the heaviness of water entailed small and limited tanks for feeding the steam-thrusters.

In battle, the dirigibles were used mainly for reconnaissance. The Kevlar coating protected the balloons from small-caliber gunfire, but it was tempting fate to fly too close over hostile territory. Only in emergency or the most desperate situation would an airman fly directly over a battlefield, to drop a bomb or fire a shotgun into the enemy below. Finally, each craft was equipped with a mounted crossbow. At reasonably close range, an arrow shot from the bow would pierce the shell of an enemy airship, so that dirigible dogfights occasionally occurred.

Al trained with the air force for three days, then was approved to take a dirigible aloft on his own. The hiking he had been doing for weeks gave him strong lungs and legs. He showed that he could move the blimp speedily. Rising over the Old Indiana countryside, he looked down at the huddle of houses that was the city of Piedmont. He could see the main roads coming in and out of town, with foot, bicycle, and horseback traffic flowing in steady streams. To the south lay the flat, blue mirror that was the Lake of a Thousand Acres, a body of water accurately if not so creatively named. Beyond the lake was a forest stretching another five or six miles.

In the warm sun, rising higher on a mild breeze, Al soaked in the near-silence and admired the southerly view. Then it hit him. A dirigible would be the perfect vehicle for escaping Piedmont and Piedmont's army. He pedaled slowly, memorizing the lay of the land, hatching a plan.

When Al eventually landed he saw General Piedmont standing beside the air force captain. Al was delighted that the general and captain approved his piloting. He was doubly delighted when the general shouted, "It looks like we have a new flyboy!"

11

Albert pondered: When was the best time to effect his escape?

At night the tethered dirigibles were under guard. During many afternoons the blimp pilots practiced bombing maneuvers and dogfighting, firing harmless, rubber-tipped arrows at one another's airships. Al learned that a dirigible was rarely flown alone, but in groups of at least three or four. There was the occasional spy mission, when a single pilot went aloft to survey enemy activities. There were rumors that Old Chilton, one town over from Old Piedmont and hitherto an army-less ally of Old Piedmont, had mounted and was drilling its own militia. Al hinted to his commander that aerial surveillance might be helpful. The commander agreed. But when he consulted with General Piedmont, the general advised sending a different and more seasoned airman aloft.

The blimp pilot went up one full-moonlit night and returned pedaling furiously, at all the speed he could manage. He bore alarming intelligence. Not only had Old Chilton mounted a militia, but that militia on this very night was mustering a few miles away, on the fringes of Piedmont County's largest watermelon patch. Dusty Longsinger was present when General Piedmont received the news. Afterward, he reported to Al that the general pronounced the Old Chilton militia's movements "insidious" and immediately deduced the militia's designs. Each summer Old Chilton hosted a five-day watermelon festival. This spring they had lost their largest melon patch to the blight. To save and properly equip this midsummer's festival, the general surmised, they had improper designs on Old Piedmont's melons. Quickly word spread through the barracks, to soldiers recreating at the town bar: tomorrow morning the Piedmont Army would march, and would fight for the honor of Piedmont and its most prized melons.

The army bustled with the excitement of imminent combat. But one soldier—Private Airman Albert Simmel, a.k.a. the Waffle Killer—thought of other possibilities than saving Piedmont County's watermelons. With Dusty Longsinger's assistance, the night before battle he hid his backpack of supplies in the dirigible he would be flying the next day.

❧

General Piedmont's army marched at dawn. Al and one other airman—Lieutenant Rusty Holcomb—were sent aloft. Al's heart wasn't in the impending battle. He concentrated on his quest for Valerie. But he had to admit that the army made quite a picture from a vantage point above the treetops. In the lead, with four red bandanas bristling on his arm, and erect with sword drawn and rested at his shoulder, General Piedmont rode proudly on a white stallion. Godfrey, the army's canine mascot, trotted alongside. Directly behind the general and his dog were ten more men on horseback, their horses nervously prancing and rearing slightly with their sensing of their riders' excitement. After the cavalry stepped the thirty soldiers comprising the infantry. As Al observed, their march was brisk and their lines were true, excepted only by sharply sidestepped detours around a pile of horse apples freshly deposited on the roadway. And at the rear of the advancing forces? Two wagons bearing fireworks, the light artillery to be deployed at this engagement.

Arrived a few hundred yards from the watermelon patch, the army stopped. Lieutenant Holcomb was sent ahead to assess the forces arrayed against Old Piedmont's bravest. The lieutenant pedaled vigorously, then, above the lip of the patch, he executed a slow, sweeping curve, making his count. Rifle shots popped in the early morning air, the Old Chilton militia assuring Holcomb would not linger over their heads. Holcomb's zeppelin swung back toward the Old Piedmont encampment, with a couple of steambursts released to speed from its dangerous proximity to the enemy. Al manipulated switch-valves and lowered his ship until it bobbed only ten feet over the heads of the Piedmont infantry. Holcomb likewise descended as he glided to a spot above General Piedmont.

"Your report, soldier," the general barked.

"Sir, yes sir!" Holcomb shouted. "Their forces are more impressive than we anticipated, sir. There are at least sixty militiamen, sir!"

General Piedmont attempted a stoic impassivity, but his mount detected his surprise and danced sideways. The general reined the horse still. "Cavalry, dismount!" The cavalrymen did as ordered. Piedmont stayed in the saddle, the better to address his entire army. He raised his voice to be heard by all.

"We are outnumbered, men. The enemy bests us by at least fifteen soldiers. To initially engage with a charge would be stupid and more costly than necessary. We will commence first with artillery to drive from the field as many of their troops as we can."

A colonel raised his hand. "Permission to speak, sir!"

The general nodded.

"The watermelons are planted between rows of corn, sir. The stalks are dry and with our artillery we are likely to start a fire, sir. And roast our melons, sir!"

"Exactly," said Piedmont. "Sometimes you must destroy a watermelon patch in order to save it."

Al recognized the line as a paraphrase of an infamous line from the twentieth-century war the US fought in Vietnam. A soldier had declared, "Sometimes you must destroy a village in order to save it." The general betrayed no knowledge of the earlier declaration and, with his next order, banished any possibility that he was speaking ironically.

"Infantry, advance two hundred yards and mount the artillery!"

Infantrymen scrambled. First several planted forked sticks in the ground. Others dashed to the wagons and returned from them to the stick mounts. The firework cannonades were laid sideways, their business ends pointed at the watermelon patch and the Old Chilton militia. Hovering above, Al looked on a line of two dozen of the cannonades, spread across a distance of seventy-five yards. The general called for ignition of the fireworks. Soldiers dropped to one knee, flicked cigarette lighters at the wicks of each of the fireworks, then hustled back fifteen or twenty paces.

A cardboard and paper mortar directly beneath Al fired first. With a resounding pop, a sizzling ball belched forth. Then a second cannonade flared down the line, followed immediately by a third at the far end from Al.

It seemed that all the fireworks were instantaneously launching their loads. Thick white smoke enveloped the entire line. Red, green, and blue fireballs arced toward the watermelon patch. Some fell short of the patch, but a half-dozen or more flew all the way home to their targets. The Old Chilton militiamen were stunned at the gunpowder charges suddenly dropped into their midst. They dashed for cover as fireballs hissed like a nest of angry snakes, and bounced off cornstalks in broken circles.

"Mmmmm-POP! Zzzzzz-BANG!" sounded the fireworks. The fireballs kept coming, careening crazily into the watermelon patch. Al raised his airship to a quarter-mile's altitude to lift beyond the gushing smoke. He could see that the Old Chilton militiamen had abandoned the field. More ominously, at least three fires had started in the melon patch. Flames licked out and then ravenously leapt across rows of the parched cornstalks. Within minutes the entire patch was ablaze. Dark smoke rolled from it. Conflagrations ignited from separate locations ran together and consolidated their heat and fire.

Al and Holcomb shouted down the news that Old Chilton had abandoned the field. General Piedmont called for his men to extinguish the now very considerable blaze in the melon patch. Several soldiers ran toward the patch, but quickly ascertained that fire had engulfed the entire patch and was beyond any means at their disposal for stopping it. The soldiers drew near enough to hear the flames crackling noisily. Their heat drove the soldiers back. Burning cornstalks broke with a sound like tree limbs splintering. Melons swelled and exploded and their red, mostly liquid meat boiled. An acrid but somewhat sweetened odor pervaded the air.

Accepting the futility of fighting the fire, the general called for his men to stand down. From his vantage point aloft, Al saw the general retreat to a ditch. The general turned his back to his forces and began relieving himself. Godfrey padded into the ditch beside the general, corkscrewed a full turn once, twice, then hiked a rear leg.

❧

It was when Al saw Lieutenant Holcomb lower his zeppelin, and throw out an anchoring cable to land, that he decided. Now was the time to make his escape. General Piedmont and his army were distracted. Al kept what money he had on himself at all times. He had his pack stowed in the airship. The only drawback with running now was not getting to say goodbye to Dusty Longsinger.

Al turned his dirigible south and pedaled briskly. His mistake was probably hitting the steam thrusters, for then the dirigible shot forward at twice its usual speed, and caught the eye of soldiers on the ground. Al heard someone shout, "Where's the Waffle Killer going?" He looked down and behind, and saw a soldier pointing up at him. Within seconds Holcomb waved away soldiers who had grabbed his anchoring cable. With the cable still dangling beneath his dirigible, the lieutenant rose quickly back up in the air, and hit his steam thrusters full blast. He was in hot pursuit.

Al had a lead on Holcomb, but Holcomb had more experience piloting. Holcomb left his steam thrusters wide open, which both helped him rapidly close distance on Al and, by releasing all water from the tank, lightened his balloon's load. Al mistakenly thought he should conserve some steam power and pedaled furiously but with a heavier load.

Holcomb zoomed within fifty yards of Al and began launching arrows from his crossbow. One arrow whizzed within a few feet of Al's head. That gave him enough adrenaline to keep him pedaling all out. The canny lieutenant jetted to a higher altitude than Al. He knew the Kevlar coating on the balloons was thinner on top than on their bottoms—after all, most shots at the balloons would come from the ground below them.

Al realized Holcomb was attempting downward shots, at the less protected topside of his aircraft. He hit the switch-valves, but just as his balloon began to rise he heard a sickening sound. There was a muffled thud as an arrow struck his dirigible, then a loud hissing. Almost immediately Al's ship began dropping.

The trees that had looked small and distant quickly enlarged in his vision and seemed to rush up at Al. He looked ahead and saw a large barn. He steered toward it and pedaled faster. The front edge of the balloon skidded on the barn's roof. Al grabbed his backpack and leapt from the pilot's cage. He laid flat to slow his slide on the roof and fortunately came to a stop still well on the very slight pitch that fanned out from the roof's peak.

Suddenly relieved of its pilot's weight, Al's dirigible bobbed upward. Holcomb stopped pedaling and braked with his rudder-flaps to keep from colliding with Al's balloon. Now Al was on his feet, eyeing the anchor cable that whipped under Holcomb. Al grabbed at the cable but missed. He had the length of the barn's roof in which to gain the cable. He jogged forward and, disastrously, slipped on a loose shingle. He went to his knees, scurried back to his feet and saw the cable about to drag off the far end of the roof.

Al sprinted the remaining length of the roof and saw the anchoring cable leave the roof just a foot from his grasp. In a split second, he realized both that he would not be able to stop himself from going over the edge of the barn's top, and that his final chance at catching the cable was to leap off the edge after it. He took two more running steps and launched into the open air.

He hit the cable high, which was fortunate because he got hold with one hand but slid downward until he managed a grip with both hands. He jerk-swung on the rope like a crazy pendulum. The upper branches of a towering Oak tree suddenly shot up before him. Al squeezed the rope tighter and felt the branches scratching and grabbing at his shins. He held tight and swung free.

Ground rushed by forty feet below Al, then he was hurtling over a bright blue and greenish surface. He realized they were over the Lake of a Thousand Acres. He clambered up the rope. Holcomb looked over the edge of the pilot's cage, now aware that Al was climbing toward him. It was apparent that he could hardly believe Al had caught the rope.

Al capitalized on the lieutenant's confusion. He completed his climb and grabbed the side bar of the pilot's cage. This tipped the cage—and Holcomb—toward him. Al clutched at the collar of Holcomb's jacket with his left arm, holding on to the cage's sidebar with his right. Holcomb bellowed and flailed, but he was already going over the cage's bar. His headfirst momentum yanked him from the cage. Al saw Holcomb tumble and fall into the water, then swung himself into the pilot's seat.

He heard the lieutenant cussing him as he adjusted the switch-valves and rose higher. He pedaled, vigorously at first, but then Holcomb was a small dark spot in the lake and Al eased into a slower yet steady pedaling rhythm.

He had made it. He checked for the sun's position and corrected the dirigible's course slightly to head due south. He would ride the balloon until he was too hungry and thirsty, or had arrived at the town in northern Old Kentucky, where he would find instructions to take him farther down the path to Valerie. Permitting himself a momentary celebration, he laid his head back in the cage and whooped.

12

In the act of his desertion, the one object of any real value that Al left behind was a pocket Bible. He supposed he would find another one soon, in the course of his travels. But in the meantime he would miss regularly reading from it.

This absence reminded Al that the Christian faith was a mediated faith, a treasure passed down from generation to generation. The squandrels for a while had imagined they could have faith without any mediating institutions such as the church or "organized religion." They spoke of being spiritual but not religious, meaning they supposed their faith was directly the individual's own, with God found in their "hearts" and their private reading of the Bible. Poke McNearland poked fun at these idle suppositions. What was the opposite of "organized religion," he said, but disorganized religion? In imagining that they could properly read the Bible apart from the church and some real connection to apostolic and creedal faith, these squandrels wasted tradition and the hard-earned resources of history just as recklessly as they despoiled and cast aside natural resources.

On these matters Father McNearland liked to cite the original Protestant, Martin Luther. The Reformer, who after all did not throw away all of his Catholic faith, affirmed that the living Christ could be found in all of creation—"in stone, in fire, in water, for he certainly is there." Yet without an interpretive key or guide Christ's presence in creation could be overlooked or mistaken. So Christ does not wish that we seek him "apart from the Word," said Luther. He does not leave us groping about for him, with each generation or individual believer consigned to remaking the faith anew. How dreadful that would be, Father McNearland said, always starting from scratch, forever blundering through a spiritual trial and error, over and over again reinventing the wheel of faith. Far better, with Luther, to lean on the church and its traditions and rightly discern Christ in the Word and the sacraments, where we may "lay hold of him in the right way."

Such, at any event, were Al's theological musings as he tramped through a corner of the state of Old Kentucky. Deep into the month of June, summer was ever more forcefully asserting itself. The afternoons burned with a stifling heat. And this summer, in this part of the world, had been drought-dry. The toasted, yellowed grass crunched beneath Al's boots. Before and beside his strides, grasshoppers exploded and flew from the ground like popping corn. The grasshoppers came in all sizes. Some were tiny. Others were huge, almost as large as a woman's little finger. Occasionally Al would grab one of the insects as it bounded near his hands. Held between his fingers, the grasshopper would spit out a thick brown liquid that exactly resembled tobacco juice.

The grasshoppers were the most plentiful living things in Al's path, but occasionally he flushed a scrawny jackrabbit from hiding. On a couple of occasions he saw coyotes at some distance. In the cloudless sky above him there were hawks, crows, sparrows, and higher above, now and then, turkey buzzards sweeping in wide circles like those marking a radar screen.

❧

After traveling in a southerly direction for several weeks, from a designated church member to the one he was pointed to in the next town, Al was now being steered west. From dilapidated road signs, he knew he was proceeding on the ruins of what had been Interstate 64, ahead merging into 70. Occasionally there were trains from city to city, and he would ride to rest and cover miles faster. Sometimes, for the same purpose, he rode riverboats for a spell. He still did not know where his final destination, and Valerie, would be. He wondered if he would push west all the way into Old Colorado, and felt a pull in his stomach at the prospect of seeing the Rocky Mountains, towering behemoths of stone and lumber he had only seen pictured in atlases and travel books in libraries. But he knew a trip into the mountains would be arduous and time-consuming, and hoped he wouldn't have to go west into Old Colorado.

On the other hand, the church network that had spirited Valerie to safety (please God!) might soon direct him south again. He reckoned that he could end up in what used to be Old Texas, but was now the Republic of Texas. Old Texas was the one state successful in seceding from the USA.

Many citizens of Old America considered the Republic of Texas arrogant and contrary and selfish, and referred to it by its unfortunate acronym—ROT. Inhabitants of Texas, then, were Rotters. Originally, of course, Texas Republicans (as they liked to call themselves) despised the ROT and Rotters designations. But eventually, in the mysterious fashion by which a people adopt a name initially used to ridicule them, the Texans claimed the names for themselves and became proud Rotters.

Al was ambivalent at the prospect of entering the Republic of Texas. There was a certain romance attached to travel in the ROT, due to its wildness and danger. The downside of wildness and danger, though, was that they were wild and dangerous. For instance, Rotters had revived the antiquated code of duello. Rotter men (and women, too, in an egalitarian departure from the earlier code) were constantly perceiving actionable offenses in even the mildest of slights, and calling someone to bring a pistol out to duel in the streets. Al had talked at length with a traveler who had spent time in the ROT. "The dogs and cats have gunfights down there," he said.

Obviously, travel in Old America presented dangers long before one crossed the border into the ROT. Not least threateningly, road bandits might lurk at many spots along the way. With such realities in mind, Al had brought along the rifle mounted in the cage of the Old Piedmont Army's dirigible. (The .22 that he had earlier traveled with had been confiscated by the Old Piedmont militia.) He hoped to heaven he never had to use it on a person, but rested in the certainty that in any event a clearly armed sojourner was less likely to be attacked than an unarmed one. So, he thought, he had traded a Bible for a gun. What deadly traditions, what violent customs, were embodied in the rifle's long blue barrel, its gleaming wood stock and trigger and firing hammer? If guns could talk, they would recite histories of tragedy, of countless men, women, and children shot down in war and swept into oblivion on rivers of their own blood. They would speak of crazed friends and enemies, spouses and feuding neighbors, riddled by bullets in the sanctity of their own homes. And they would tell stories, too, of gallantry and regret, of being taken up and fired reluctantly and ending or preventing even greater violence.

❧

Eventually Al found himself west of Old St. Louis, on Interstate 70. He was next to go to the First Presbyterian Church in Old Florissant, and ask there for Elder John Edgar Widdenfeld. He located the town and then the church, and found its pastor in his study. The pastor directed him to a café a few blocks away, where at this time of day John Edgar Widdenfeld would be enjoying his supper.

At the café, a query to a waitress enabled Al to determine that Elder Widdenfeld was the trim, grayheaded gentleman alone in a booth, tucking into a meal of steak and eggs. Widdenfeld was friendly even before Al offered the network's passcode. He was positively hospitable after Al quietly spoke the code to him. The old man gave the code response, breathlessly, hurriedly, then insisted that Al sit and join him. Before Al could say another word, John Edgar hollered in a friendly tone at his waitress. "Katy, another plate of steak and eggs, for my friend." He pointed a butter knife at Al. "And another basket of those dinner rolls, please and thank you, my dear."

Not wanting to appear ungrateful, Al summoned patience and ate most of his steak—and three truly delicious dinner rolls—before he became insistent that his voluble new friend let him know what was the town and church he should next visit.

"Of course, of course, you do want to know that, above all. I understand." Widdenfeld put down his fork and wiped a napkin across his lips. "And that girl, your Valerie, I know you're eager to find her. I don't want to see her or you disappointed."

He offered up the pertinent information, then had Al rehearse the information back to him.

"There, you have it," said Widdenfeld. "Now, it's getting late in the day. I insist that you stay the night. My lovely bride and I have a guest room. And of all the luck, your timing is impeccable. It is movie night at the Marquee, the house of cinema in our village. Have you seen *The Wizard of Oz*? It is one of our town favorites, and on the bill tonight."

Al in fact had seen only three or four movies in his entire lifetime. The energy constraints of the Age of the Descent meant that no new movies were made, and that the exhibition of old films was affordable only to the wealthy constituents. The price of a movie ticket amounted to several months' salary for a sub. So it was the very special and very rare occasion that subs saw a movie. That said, Al had thoroughly enjoyed the handful of movies he's seen. He hated to miss this opportunity, but told Widdenfeld he could never afford a ticket. Widdenfeld laughed and replied that the town showed movies for free, "as an act of civic courtesy, entertainment, and service." Al's spirits leapt. He had read the book on which the film was based, and his Granddad Madison dreamily mused about movies and movie theaters that were still more regularly available in his early childhood.

Widdenfeld seemed to sense Al's excitement and suddenly his face went sober. "I should inform you, however, that tonight's showing will be a bittersweet affair. We use a generator to power the projector, and for years have saved fuel to run the generator once a week. But we are just about run out of fuel, and tonight will be our final movie showing. When the screen goes black tonight—and I hate to say this, my friend—it will go black for the last time." Rather selfishly, Al caught himself thinking that he would not be around for next week's movie anyway. How lucky he was to have happened into this town on this night. He could hardly wait for showtime.

Finally the hour arrived and Al walked with the elder to the Marquee Theater, some five blocks distant from the café. The streets were bustling, with men and women who could not help but walk faster and faster in anticipation, with the shouts and gleeful squeals of children who had not yet learned to conceal their animal excitement. The theater itself was a white-stuccoed structure, rectangular and plain except for three arches behind which the ticket booth stood. There were faded movie posters on the outside walls flanking the ticket booth. People were flowing inside the theater eagerly but politely, now taking their small children by the hand so that they wouldn't be lost or trampled in the crowd, or bowl over some esteemed elderly citizen with their dashes into the delicious darkness of the auditorium.

Al was not disappointed once he and Elder Widdenfeld were inside and seated. They took a seat near the back, and the raked floor swept before them, careening all the way to the screen and its frame. The floors were sticky with decades of soda syrup residue. Al felt underneath his seat and, as his grandfather had remarked, found fossilized globs of chewing gum. He thought about the generations of children and lovers that had huddled before this screen, witnessing a fantastic array of worlds. Cops and robbers. Cowboys and Indians. Earthlings and aliens. On the screen, he imagined and hearkened to his grandfather's memory, people made love and were born and died, and fought with blows that landed with a sound like cannons shot. On the screen brave, handsome men time after time rose to every challenge presented them. Beautiful women shone, haloed in soft focus, their faces thirty feet high and finer than any architecture. All the while, swelling, lush music played by the best orchestras in the world flooded the air.

And then, in the Marquee, the house lights went down. Grown men and women squealed and clapped and hooted. And from behind and above them, a tunnel of light appeared, almost solid with suspended dust motes, and at the same instant the screen fired and glowed to life.

The theater was a kind of cave, Al thought. People retreated into it as if it were a primordial shelter that would protect them from the worries and troubles of the outside world. The fire on this cave's hearth pulsated with pictures, images not in shadows, as Plato conceived, but in full color and as clear in their details as the features of a stream bottom beneath icy clean water.

Of course, *The Wizard of Oz* did not begin in color. Dorothy's home of Kansas was black and white, if punctuated by curiosities such as a traveling medicine man and excitement such as house-hurling tornadoes. But soon enough, when Dorothy landed in the magical land of Oz, the screen was alive with Technicolor. Al gasped along with others in the audience. The rich, saturated hues, with each frame painterly in its composition, were more real and more luxurious than anything outside the theater.

Most of the viewers here, unlike Al, had seen *The Wizard of Oz* before. But no one seemed tired of it or callously inured to its magic. Screams rang out with the flying monkeys swooped down on Dorothy and her winsome companions. Approving yells and applause marked the melting and steaming away as the Wicked Witch collapsed beneath her black garments.

The movie proceeded in all its wonder of story and characterization and distillation of light. But then . . .

But then, just as the wizard's balloon broke from its moorings and he floated away waving his top hat, the picture on the screen hitched and hiccupped. It sludged into slow motion and went dark for a moment, then fired back to life, but jerkily. And only momentarily. The tunnel of light died and vanished altogether. The auditorium dropped into pitch-blackness and the citizens of Old Florissant, watching their very last movie, fell utterly silent. The generator, prematurely, had run out of fuel.

Seconds passed, with hopes crashed and bitter realization dawning. Then a child cried out, "But Mommy, Mommy! Does Dorothy get back home again?"

13

Back on the road, Al missed his father. By the nature of the case with Valerie's secretive flight, Al did not know how much farther he had to go before he found her. That uncertainty, plus the fact that he was now several weeks into the trip, pushed him into impatience. He thought about how much faster he would move if he had a horse. But that possibility clamped him in a double bind. He had insufficient funds to buy a horse, so he would have to work somewhere and earn some money. And that would mean stopping in one place and laboring there for probably a month.

In all events, his mind was on horses, and that soon enough led to thoughts of his father, who loved and worked with horses all his life. Al was not proud of it, but he still bore hard feelings toward his dad. Their estrangement had not been clearly overcome before Ray Simmel's death. With Ray on his deathbed, Al did speak aloud that he loved him, but when his supposedly comatose dad responded with a squeeze of Al's hand, Al was so startled that he jerked his hand loose from his father's grip. Looking back, he could hope and pray that his father had understood that the spoken words were sincere, and the yanking away of his hand involuntary and reflexive, the result of surprise.

But that hand squeeze was Ray Simmel's last earthly attempt to grip his son. Family life was complicated, it seemed, and in no small part because its intimacy and intensity entailed negotiating a series of grips. A man and a woman in love grip each other, and out of their grip comes a child. When the child is very young, he requires constant gripping by his parents—the handholds that lift him from a crib, that sit him down for a meal, that pull him up when he falls down, that stop him when he ventures too near a fire. The nature of the gripping changes as the child ages. He will not mature unless his parents learn when they must loosen their grips. They will inevitably make mistakes in these complex discernments, sometimes holding on too long, at other times realizing, in stinging retrospect, that that they let go too soon. Loving and smart parents can only learn how to be appropriately gripping parents through repeated practice. And, for better or worse, the only ones they practice parenting are their own children.

For the child's part, he must learn to appreciate a parent's grip when it is fitting and will truly help him, but also tug to break grips that are overprotective or smothering. Usually he will not even remotely begin to understand how he was gripped by his parents, and how hard their task was, until after he becomes an adult.

This musing on grips dug up one of Al's earliest memories. He was four or five. Out for a winter walk with his father, Al dashed onto a frozen river. But it was not far enough into winter to be sure of the ice's thickness and firmness. Ray yelled for his son to stop, but Al was learning how to tug against his parents' grips, and he toddled at least twenty feet on to the ice before he stopped and turned to look at his father. The sensations that happened next were vivid in Al's memory.

He remembered his breath steaming out from his mouth when he started to shout "No!" back at his father. Then suddenly he dropped. One moment he saw his father's face and snow-sheeted trees behind him. The next moment everything was roiling and murky. Frigid water immediately and violently swept into his nose and open mouth. He tried to yell, and sucked in even more water. He kicked and flailed, and suddenly his surroundings were darker. Beneath the ice, he had forced himself away from the hole opened by his fall. Below was blackness, above was a gray mass, seemingly here solid as concrete and interlaced with bubbles and streaks of white. Panic consumed him. His thrashing rotated him in the water and on the third or fourth rotation a sight forced itself through the panic into consciousness. Not too far away a column of light plunged into the water. In the column was an arm and a groping hand. He did not so much think "Dad!" as his whole body cried it out and churned him toward his father's hand. His father's grip.

Ray Simmel had bellied onto the ice to distribute his weight and keep himself from falling through the ice. He pulled his son out of the water, then dragged him across the ice to the riverbank. In freezing temperatures, they were at least ten minutes from home. Ray Simmel yanked his son out of the soaked clothes, then wrapped him in Ray's own coat and shirt. He even ripped off his gloves and jammed his son's small hands into them.

Exposed, he ran, carrying Al to warmth and safety. His actions saved his son from all but a case of the sniffles, but resulted in frostbite to the arm and hand he had, without hesitation, stabbed into the icy water after his son. He lost the tip of the little finger on his right hand.

And now when Al remembered the second grip, the grip of his father on his deathbed, he saw the hand with the abbreviated finger. That was the hand, the grip, Al had pulled away from in surprise and fright at his father's deathbed. He wished now he had rested in that last grip, and held on to it as tightly as he did to the grip that saved him from a toddler's demise. But he was still learning to be a son at the same time his father was learning to be a father. He could and he thought he should regret jumping away from that last fatherly grip. But regret was a bitter and futile cup. What else could he possibly have done?

❧

Around noon, the sun burning directly above him, Al arrived on the outskirts of a town called Girardsville. There was a tension in the air. People approaching him on the sidewalk refused to meet his gaze and passed him mutely. Soon enough he realized they weren't even talking to each other. And they moved urgently, walking fast and barely suppressing sprints, dragging along dawdling children like unbroken puppies on a leash. Al had a nagging sense that something was awry, that it might be best to turn around, exit the town, and walk around it with a wide berth.

But before he made up his mind he came upon an intersection where policemen were stopping all traffic, pedestrian or vehicular. Apparently the lawmen were inspecting identification credentials. Whatever exactly the papers might be Al knew he had no such credentials. It was too late, however, to break away from the intersection. Two of the four cops had already caught sight of him and were glancing his way.

The line in front of Al advanced rapidly. As he drew nearer to the cops' blockade, he saw people flashing blue cards and being sent on their way. The few words exchanged between the police and the detained made clear that the blue cards proved their citizenship in Girardsville.

Soon enough Al was at the head of the line. With a vaguely menacing air, a cop slapped a billy club against his cupped hand. He addressed Al: "You don't look familiar. Identification?"

"I'm not from here. I don't have one of those blue cards."

The cop arched an eyebrow. Al was feeling more and more nervous.

"I'd be happy to get one," he said, "if you'll just tell me where to go."

The cop smiled grimly and turned to his fellow officers. "Look here, boys. We got ourselves a stranger, a gen-u-wine alien." The other officers came alive, with grins and backslaps. Then the first one said, "Turn around, son, and we'll cuff you."

"Wait just a minute!" Al said. "What have I done wrong?" He shook loose of the cop who had grabbed him by the elbow. Then, faster than thought, the four surrounded him. The cop directly behind Al kicked him in the back of the knees and Al crumpled. Then one on Al's left put his foot on Al's back and pushed him flat on the ground. A third grabbed Al's wrists, twisted them behind his back, and applied the handcuffs—seemingly all in one motion. Al was still protesting, if more quietly, when two of the cops hauled him to his feet. Then, like a snakebite, the first cop's billy club struck across Al's face. His nose was bloodied and his lip cut. He felt the warm blood streaming into his mouth and tasted its saltiness. He was stunned and groggy, but he understood enough to cease all resistance and protestations.

The policemen threw Al into the back of a horse-drawn wagon. Then one took the reins and one—the billy-clubber—climbed into the back of the wagon beside Al. The other two cops stayed behind as the horse's iron shoes clopped along the broken asphalt streets. The wagon jostled and bumped over potholes, bouncing Al on the wooden bed and making the heartily applied and tightened handcuffs dig further into his wrists.

The wagon covered a few blocks before it was clear they were entering the center of the town. Vehicular traffic thickened. The clots of pedestrians grew more dense and numerous. Onlookers began to taunt Al. Two boys on the back of a passing wagon threw eggs at Al. The sidewalks hummed with an ominous, susurrus hiss. "He's brought evil among us!" someone shouted. Another jeered, "The devil's goat!" This taunt was repeated and began to gain momentum, until there was a loud chorus, up and down the street. "The devil's goat! The devil's goat!"

Al was thoroughly frightened. Two minutes before he would have been unable to imagine the cops as friends, but now he sensed them as the only boundary between himself and the increasingly frenzied mob. The policeman at the reins shooed the horses and quickened their pace. Presently they rolled up to the back of a small, red-bricked jailhouse. The billy-clubber hustled Al out of the wagon and into one of the three cells inside.

He shoved Al face-first against the wall and brusquely removed the cuffs, taking skin with them as they came off.

The barred door clunked shut with heavy iron force. Al collapsed onto the disheveled bunk. Outside the jeering continued, for what seemed hours, before he was overcome with desperate exhaustion and drifted into a troubled sleep.

☙

He awoke to find a figure in a black cassock sitting on a stool. The man was finishing a cigarette. When he saw Al's eyes were open and had focused on him, he opened his fingers and dropped the cigarette to the floor. For some reason, he did not grind it out, so the cigarette lay smoldering, a gentle, rippling stream of smoke rising into the late evening light of the cell.

"Hello, my name is William Gration." He swung his palms apart, in the sweeping "Viola!" gesture of a magician. "Father William Gration."

Al said nothing.

Gration said, "You are probably wondering what you are doing here?"

Al thought this so obvious a question that he saw no need to reply. Gration had the mien of an office manager who has already decided what he wants his charges to do, but attempts to manipulate them into believing they want the same, and had even come up with the idea. This grated. Al remained mute.

"All right," said Gration. "Let's get directly to the point. What shall I call you?"

"Simmel, I'm Albert Simmel."

"All right, 'Simmel-I'm-Albert-Simmel,' please allow me to address you as Simmel."

He paused again, as if Al was expected to greet this magnanimous decision with eager ardor. Sore of head, wrists, and back, Al wanted to slap the man. But he knew he was in deep trouble and that insolence would not help. He grunted in response.

Gration resumed, "There have troubles in our burg lately, Simmel. I am the chief priest and leader of Girardsville. Our town consists of fifteen clans, fifteen extended families and their, shall we say, retainers. As chief priest my job is to keep the peace between the clans. Do you know the one thing that tears communities apart more than any other?"

Al was beginning to get intrigued, despite himself and Gration's annoying manner. He shook his head no.

"It is envy, Simmel, envy pure and simple. What are worries about justice and equality except envy that one will have more money or power or sex or whatever than another? Why do those who are rich insist they have earned every bit of the wealth they possess and that those without wealth deserve their privation? Because they know the corrosive, acidic, madly energizing power of envy. And they know how good it feels to be envied. They want to ride atop turbulent waves of envy, peering down from the heights of their superior status, and at the same time secure their status by insisting the world will be as it already is. Rich and poor alike are in their places."

"Look, this is interesting," said Al. "But what has this got to do with me? I'm not even from here."

"Ah! Exactly. You're not from here. And that is why you can help us with our troubles. Let me put just a bit finer a point on my little mediation about envy."

Al leaned back against the wall above his bunk and released a sigh of concession.

"What do you suppose is the most complicated sort of envy?"

"I don't know," Al said.

"All right, all right, Simmel. I see that you tire of my Socratic method of explanation. I'll stop putting my explanation in the form of questions."

"Thank you," Al said.

The chief priest ignored the hint of sarcasm.

"Envy is most complicated when two (or more) parties want exactly the same thing, and there is no way more than one can have it. It's one thing to envy wealth. As long as there's some wealth to go around, others can share in the wealth and lose their envy of the wealthy. It's one thing for a woman or a man to be envious of another's sex appeal, but as long as there are other possible mates to go around, the envious can abate their envy.

"But consider the more complicated form of envy. If two women want exactly the same man, the envy of the loser cannot abate. If two or more of our clans want to be the wealthiest clan in town, then there can be only one winner and the rest can only burn with envy.

"This tendency runs very deep. Think of two children playing. One has a ball, another has a toy car. The one with the toy car has no interest in the ball until he sees the other child enjoying the ball. Then he, too, wants the ball. It does not even help to present a second ball. The child wants the very same ball his playmate possesses. His desire is imitative.

"The same thing happens, if sometimes more subtly, among adults. There can only be one chief priest in this town, so others are bound to envy my chief priesthood. Egalitarian as we try to be, some clans are inevitably richer than others, or have more representatives on our council of elders, or have more handsome men and beautiful women, and so on and so on. We keep peace, or some semblance of peace, over long stretches of time. But then the festering envies explode.

"As I said, Girardsville has lately come upon dark times. Robberies are at levels we haven't seen for decades. Four or five clans have descended into gang wars. Their violence has escalated and turned uglier and uglier. So the Brumley clan started scalping their murdered enemies. The Whitecote clan has responded by removing the genitals of their kills."

Gration shuddered. For once Al sympathized with him.

"The unease only increases when things have dropped this far. We marry across clans, and spouses have begun to question the clan loyalties of one another. Two nights ago, a fine, upstanding member of our community shot his wife because he had become convinced she was more devoted to her clan of origin than to her clan by marriage. He dug a grave in the backyard, then he shot her dog and threw it in the hole after her.

"I trust this indicates how much disharmony has pervaded our town. So how can we be united again? What can most easily and effectively draw us back together? I will tell you: it is a common enemy. If we are no longer together in what we love, we can come together in what we hate. The leaders of this community have learned that, in these situations, we need a scapegoat."

Realization—dark, panicked realization—dawned on Al.

"And that is why," said the chief priest, "that is why that tomorrow, at three o'clock in the afternoon, you will be removed from this cell. You will be paraded through a gauntlet of eight blocks, and our city will come together in hate. The crowds will concentrate hate and fear and all the diseases of envy on you. Then you will be blindfolded and gagged, and taken to a seventy-five-foot-tall tower situated in the middle of a large field. So everyone in town can and will see.

"Everyone will see you, an outsider, the devil's own goat, pushed from the top of the tower and plunging to your death. And in your death we will have life again."

THE SECOND BAPTISM OF ALBERT SIMMEL

14

It was late. The town had fallen silent, except for the occasional clopping of horses' hooves, and dogs barking themselves hoarse.

Al didn't feel like he was getting any sleep, but he realized he must be dozing on and off, because the moon had changed position in the sky between his glances out the cell window. Sometime close to midnight, a boisterous, drunk local had been forcibly installed in the cell next to Al's. The local was now snoring. But Al remained awake, and then came the voices.

Male voices, excited male voices. There were shouts:

"Come on Eve!"

"Do it for us, baby!"

"Peel it now!"

"Make it Christmas time, girl!

The local in the other cell stirred. He awakened with a belch and prolonged lipsmacking. He lay still, listening, then realized what the noise outside indicated. He kicked out from under the ratty blanket that had been draped over his legs. He clutched the bars at his cell window, and all but jumped up and down in anticipation. Presently he seemed to realize there was someone else in the cells with him.

"You from around here, buddy?"

Al answered no.

"Well, this is something you don't want to miss. Get up off that bunk and look out there," he said.

Al followed the local's instructions. He ascertained that the hubbub originated just across the alley from the jail. Semi-bright lights flooded the area. A high stone wall obstructed any other view, with red and green Christmas lights twinkling on top the wall. The twentieth-century Christmas song

"Silver Bells," in a sultry rendition with saxophones and trombones, and lots of bells, boomed from what had to be enormous speakers. Like pirates back from a successful raid, the men were lustily singing, "Silver bells, silver bells, it's strip-ping tiiime in the city."

"That is a whorehouse," the local said with a tip of his head in the direction of the lights.

Al knew that prostitution had been legalized across much of the Old USA. Resources for law enforcement, as for any other municipal necessities, were scarce. It made little sense for precious police time and money to be devoted to what were called victimless crimes. Marijuana and even hard drugs had been decriminalized as well as prostitution. Those aware of history marveled that the squandrels had devoted massive resources to a "war" against drugs, not only keeping police busy with drug busts but filling bigger and bigger prisons.

"So what exactly is going on over there?" Al asked.

"Eve," the local said, his voice filled with something bordering on awe. "Eve, who is a beauty, now, a real beauty, is going to do her trampoline routine. She does it every week. So it's Christmas not just in December, but in every month of the year. And that's why we"—and here Al's jailmate seemed to realize he was revealing considerable familiarity with the brothel and its practices—"that's why *they* took to calling her Christmas Eve."

"Uh huh," Al said, and then there was a burst of even noisier excitement from across the alley.

Bounce, and a lovely, young, and clearly physically fit blonde flew into sight above the wall.

Bounce. She was wearing red shorts and a tight green blouse.

Bounce. She began unbuttoning the top.

Bounce. She reappeared and cast aside the blouse.

Bounce, bounce, she was higher in the air and at her jump's peak gracefully executed a flip, in the process fluidly dispensing her green bra.

Bounce. She unbuttoned her shorts.

Bounce and bounce. She unzipped them.

Bounce. The shorts were sliding off.

Bounce . . . Bounce . . . Bounce! Another flip, with the shorts sliding over her legs and off her feet, at the exact moment she was upside down.

Eve was now clad only in a G-string. Her audience of men were beside themselves, cheering and throwing paper money at the performer. She executed three or four flips, then no longer popped into view above the wall. Apparently the show was over.

The local was dreamy-eyed, still clutching the window bars.

"Now, boy, you can die happy."

He glanced at Al and saw his ashen face, his aghast expression.

"Oh, man, it's just a figure of speech. But you're the devil's goat for tomorrow, aren't you? What have you done? Just leave me alone, buddy."

What had Al done? The only thing he knew he was guilty of was being a stranger. It appeared he might get some answers to his questions when, just after dawn, a uniformed police official came to his cell door.

"Sir," said Al, after the policeman had introduced himself, "what am I accused of doing? Did I violate curfew? Smoke the wrong brand of cigar? What?"

"Don't make light, Simmel. And don't waste your time pretending you don't know what you've done. All of your type act innocent and surprised."

"But I am innocent and surprised."

"Like I say, son, don't waste your time. We have three witnesses who saw you in the Bainbridge neighborhood early yesterday afternoon."

"Yesterday afternoon? I didn't even arrive in town until evening."

The policeman now raised his voice—and temper. "Now you're wasting my time, prisoner. You're only adding lies to lies. The fact is we have two witnesses who saw you leading a nine-year-old girl into the Bainbridge Woods."

"I did nothing with a girl! Or anyone else . . ."

"Shut up! I told you I don't want to hear your lies. The girl came home later in the day, in a ripped dress. She told her parents that a strange man—a man who fits your description—lured her into the woods and violated her. The girl's name, not that scum like you would care, is Sharon Tooley."

Al protested his innocence all the more vigorously, desperately. The cop waved away the protests and seemed to grow increasingly angry. Finally, he said, "Look, I'm just here to let you know, not that you deserve the favor, that you're going to be executed this afternoon. The evil you've brought to this town must be dispelled."

"Executed? Executed?" Al said. "Do I get a lawyer? Won't there be a trial?"

"Playing soft on criminals is bullshit, and only encourages more acts of evil. We need to vanquish, to destroy, you and your evil as quickly as we can. So save your breath. You've got just a few hours of breathing left, anyway."

The policeman departed, backing out of the cell and away from Al like he was a source of deadly and highly infectious contagion. Al refused a proffered breakfast, and later lunch. He had no stomach for food. His thoughts ran wild, full of self-incriminations that he had entered the town rather than going around it, stark fears of dying. He cursed what appeared his bitter fate. Now he would never see Valerie again, at least not in this world. And his child, the daughter or son that Valerie had probably borne. In the midst of this anxious, overwhelming rush of thoughts, Al managed to pray, feebly. He prayed for justice, for some kind of escape. Yet he doubted God's response; God had let him be shanghaied and abandoned him at this pass. Why set him out on this hard journey, and have it end now, with Al's quest ended in futility, his hands empty of any gain, with Valerie never again in his arms? Why be killed and buried in an unknown town? Why or how would God intervene now? Al watched the sun rise higher into the sky and willed it to rise more slowly. He tried to quiet his fears, a least a bit, and pray for courage and even the tiniest beginnings of forgiveness he knew Christians were supposed to return to their persecutors. In the end his efforts were mainly failures. He could send up only the most primal, basic, one-word prayer: "Help!" The Holy Spirit (if there was a Holy Spirit) would have to lift his leaden, broken prayers to God.

Time itself twisted into a kind of horrible fantasia. On the one hand it seemed to pass too quickly, with Al longing for more hours, then more minutes and seconds, before he died. On the other hand, time dragged, hobbled and weighed down by an unendurable anxiety: let's just get this over and done, Al thought.

Suddenly—or was it finally?—four policeman appeared. They shackled Al hands and feet, then led him outside. While still in the cell, Al had heard the murmurings of a crowd outside the jail. Now he was led into that mob, and the mob terribly came alive. "Devil's goat, devil's goat," it chanted. There were scattered calls:

"Kill him!"

"Evil dies. Destroy evil among us."

"God save us!"

"Expel! Expel! Expel!"

Spittle struck Al in the face repeatedly, its sour taste running into his mouth. Two or three onlookers managed to bruisingly prod Al with sticks they had apparently brought just for that purpose. But in the main the police protected Al, brandishing pistols, poking fiercely with billy clubs at the surging crowd, shouting curses. At last they arrived at a wagon with an open bed. The two horses hitched to the wagon were spooked by the mob, so that the wagon drivers struggled to keep the horses still, so that the wagon jerked forward, then backward. Al's escort at first pulled him forward and backward, trying to synchronize his loading onto the wagon with the horses' movement. Finally two of the escort simply lifted Al off his feet and tossed him like a bag of grain up and into the wagon.

The cops scrambled into the open-bedded wagon after Al. They violently hoisted him to his feet. The drivers whipped the horses and the wagon lurched ahead. The crowd, its excitement growing, surrounded the wagon and moved ahead with it. Onlookers pelted Al with rocks, and were in turn clubbed by policemen wanting to protect their colleagues who stood near Al in the wagon's bed. The volume of angry chants and calls cranked up.

Al felt horribly exposed. He might just as well be naked. He marveled at the mob's vehemence, which he had supposed was at a peak as he came out of the jail, but now ratcheted up its noise and violence by several levels. In some confused, wounded and awestruck part of himself he began to wonder if he really was guilty. How else explain the enmity of what seemed the whole world against him? He fought that sense, just as he fought to maintain interior prayers for strength. He was in all ways overwhelmed, so that he lived only moment to shocking moment. He had no past and could imagine no future, nothing like escape or rescue or even death and the pain of dying. This was what it was, he dimly realized, to be reduced to the barest essence of humanity, an animal self that can do no more than cling to life moment by moment.

The wagon arrived at an odd structure. A wooden tower rose into the air. At its top was a platform. At its bottom it was surrounded on all four sides by a concrete wall that was at least twenty feet tall. A gate swung open in the front side of the wall. Another gauntlet of policemen pushed back members of the mob who tried to follow the wagon into the tower's enclosure. As the gate swung shut, Al saw there was another high wall within the enclosure. Father Gration, again robed in black, appeared and raised Al off the ground after the cops threw him out of the wagon. "Remove yourselves," Gration said. "You know you cannot enter the holy of holies." The drivers and police escort then slipped back outside the gate, clanging it closed behind them.

Father Gration, apparently now acting as some kind of priest-executioner, then lifted Al to his feet. "Be brave," he whispered into Al's ear. Without a hint of roughness, he took Al's elbow and led him through a door inside the inner wall surrounding the tower. They mounted an elevator, which rose above the tops of the inner and the outer walls. Through the grates of the elevator, Al saw the mob, its noise tidally washing over him again. Somehow it seemed larger yet.

Once the elevator had risen to its peak, Gration opened it and led Al to the edge of an iron platform. The priest raised both hands and the crowd quieted.

"Brethren," Father Gration shouted over the mob, "evil has come into our midst."

The crowd thundered, "Expel it! Expel it!"

"Who stands before us?" the priest said, clearly now conducting a familiar liturgy.

"Devil's goat! Devil's goat!" the crowd answered.

"And if the devil's goat is vanquished?"

"Peace will come! Peace will come!" the crowd chanted.

"May God save us!" the priest yelled.

"May God save us! May God save us!" the crowd shouted back.

As the crowd continued "May God save us!" Father Gration produced a dark hood and slipped it over Al's head. An acrid, overpowering odor invaded Al's nostrils. The hood was soaked with some choking, suffocating liquid. Al lost consciousness, and as he swooned the priest pushed him forward and off the platform.

The mob roared as the body fell. Then the priest signaled for quiet, attained it, and then recited, "God has saved us! Peace has come!"

"God has saved us! Peace has come!" the crowd screamed back, over and over again.

⁂

Al's next sensation was one of sight. He was beneath a rough fabric. Light was lessened, but filtered through the material.

Al's second sensation was one of odor. The biting, overwhelming smell returned, and Al immediately felt as if he were suffocating. Was he in some inconceivable hell, where he would struggle for breath and release for an eternity? He furiously kicked and thrashed.

What was over him was a tarpaulin. It was now pulled back and Al looked up and saw clouds and blue sky. Was he then in a heaven of some kind?

"I know it's a terrible shock," a voice said from behind, at the same time that a hand was laid on Al's shoulder. Al startled and turned to face the priest.

"Am I alive?"

"You are alive," Father Gration said. "And you have not died. I know I was harsh with you yesterday, in the jail. But it was important that I maintain a certain pretense in front of your jailers. Let me now explain, more gently, what has happened to you."

"These are difficult times, as you well know," the priest began. "Communities are not easily held together even in the best of times. And one the easiest, if still difficult, ways to keep a community coherent is to give it a common enemy. Communities seem to do this almost instinctually, it seems—to look for a common enemy, I mean. At least this community, my community, seemed to do it early on in this Age of the Descent.

"I was, and I hope I may yet be, a man of God, a priest among my people. In any city, any community, there is conflict. It's unavoidable, but of course conflict can tear a city apart. Years ago, I began to notice that as tensions rose over time, it looked as if our city, Girardsville, was about to fly apart. Then one day a stranger to our town tried to rob a bank. The community was appalled, and came together around its shared hatred for this outsider robber. Not too long after that, another passerby attacked and raped one of our women. This violent crime united the community even more than the attempted bank robbery. Before the sheriff could transport the alleged rapist to higher authorities, a lynch mob formed, took the prisoner, and summarily hanged him.

"I noticed a curious but unmistakable phenomenon. Again the community drew together. And after the rapist (I think he really was guilty of the crime) was hanged, all conflict in the community lessened or disappeared. Quarreling neighbors came together in their shared appreciation that an evil man had been vanquished from amidst them. Many of the lawsuits that several had filed against their fellow citizens were dropped. Long borne grudges were forgotten. This all seemed basically to the good, though of course lynching for any crime is not to be encouraged. That way lies anarchy. At least as worse, there were a series of visitors, strangers to our city, accused of crimes it was doubtful they had committed. They too were lynched, and again a real degree of concord returned to town. As I told you yesterday, envy is a powerful force. And it abates, savagely enough, when a scapegoat is identified and the people unite against him.

"In any event, I realized that it needn't even be an actual criminal who could serve as an effective scapegoat. It had to be nothing more than a supposedly clearly evil person—and a stranger was easier to demonize than someone already familiar to our town. I preached and otherwise spoke out about the terrible trap and injustice we had fallen into. But just as a few would listen and began to agree, there would be another violent crime and a stranger accused and dispatched—I mean executed—and the catharsis, the relief people felt, especially as they rallied around our flag, so to speak, far surpassed the appeal of looking hard at the alternative. That alternative was, simply, the fact that we were ourselves criminals, we were ourselves succumbing to evil, when we killed the unjustly accused.

"What could I, a mere pastor, do? The sheriff, some judges, and others shared my anxiety and the sense that innocent strangers were dying at our hands. But they also were comforted by the peace, however tawdrily bought, that always came upon our community for some while after a scapegoat was named and dispatched. I was tempted to think that if powerful people in our legal system could venture no solution, then certainly I, nothing more than a minister, could not resist these injustices.

"But then it occurred to me. What was happening was very much a religious event. Religion, after all, is very much about holding a people together, dealing with conflicts within communities, coming together and living as one under the authority of a higher power. So it dawned on me that if what was happening was itself religious, then perhaps I should fight fire with fire. I switched my public position from one opposing the scapegoating to one in its favor. I accrued a degree of power that allowed me serious audience with the supreme judges and highest sheriff. I outlined a scheme that would allow for *apparent* executions, exactly like the one you suffered earlier today. I told my friends in high places that we would have the desired effect of apparent concord and basic peace, without convicting actually guilty strangers, and without actually killing them. So, ten years ago, they agreed to an experiment and assisted me in building the Tower of Justice.

"I know, I know, it is not truly a tower of justice, but good may come of evil, God can work with a crooked stick, and all that. The 'experiment' has reliably worked over all the years. I arranged to be a priestly executor—God forgive me—and presided alone within the inner wall, the holy of holies, as I presented it to the people. The hood I put over your head was doused in chloroform, which explains the headache you now suffer. You can imagine that I can hardly communicate to a scapegoat the complexity of my argument and scheme. What I can do, and what I in fact do, is render them unconscious and push them off the platform to their apparent death. What you, and other scapegoats, actually fall onto is effective air cushions that prevent death and any serious injuries.

"So you are alive. After you fell unconscious on the air pads, I hid you in this wagon and drove your supposed corpse out of the holy of holies to an ignominious burial of your body in an unmarked grave well outside our city limits. I can hardly expect you to thank me for putting you through this harrowing experience, but you may now go about your way in peace."

The priest laid a hand on Al's shoulder. Al looked at him, very much in a daze (and, yes, with a fierce headache). "I don't know what to tell you," he said. "I will just say that I am alive rather than dead, and I'm happy for that."

"Go on, go on now," the priest said as he gently tugged Al out of the wagon. He reached into the wagon and handed out Al's pack and money belt. He extracted a shovel from beneath the tarp. "Be on your way, quickly. And as for me, I have a faux grave to dig."

15

In the days after his near death at Girardsville, Al reflected on his "execution." What Father Gration said about envy and its ensuing violence made much sense. Al could also imagine how a succession of scapegoats brought momentary peace to a violent and divided community. But he remembered how the priest was haunted by guilt. And he thought that might be the case because Gration realized he wasn't really representing the full gospel of Jesus Christ to the people of Girardsville. Jesus himself was a sacrificial lamb—in the eyes of those who killed him, a sacrificial goat. But as the Letter to Hebrews had it, Jesus was the final sacrifice. After him and his sacrifice, there was no need or place for another sacrifice. In this sense Jesus was the last scapegoat. What would happen, Al wondered, if Father Gration preached this gospel to his people? If Jesus is the final scapegoat, there would then be no need for a succession of other scapegoats, no place for the violence of a series of blamings and (apparent) executions. Al thought of the depth and riches of the gospel and how, if understood, it could radically change people and communities.

There ensued a week or two of happily uneventful traveling. Al was somewhere in Old Missouri, moving at a brisk clip as he walked from sunup to sundown during each of the late summer days.

There were memorable, if quiet, moments. Once Al found himself surrounded by a vast field of wildflowers. The flowers throbbed in the soft golden light of late afternoon, almost neon in their hues of blue and yellow and red and purple. Al lay down for a rest. He dozed, awakened by a tickling sensation on his nose. A monarch butterfly was perched there. It took flight as he gently shook his head, but then Al noticed at least a dozen other monarchs on his chest, arms, and legs. It was a mild, almost windless day, and another couple dozen other butterflies floated in the air around

Al. Some skewed in the breeze like orange ash. One passed close by his ear, almost touching it, and the flutter of the wings at such proximity produced a "whoosh" sound, amplified like the blows in the fistfight of an old movie.

The moment of enchantment was disrupted only by Al's nagging worries about finding Val. What if the trail petered out? What if the human chain connecting him to Valerie broke and ended? What if he came to the end of this road and learned Valerie was dead? Or married to another man? He thought of John Wayne's character, Ethan, in one of the handful of movies he had seen, *The Searchers*. Ethan spent years in pursuit of a niece kidnapped by Indians. His search ended in brokenness and acrimony. Al hoped that he would not finish his search like Ethan—even if, God forbid, Al's own search ended in disappointment. But then he reflected that Ethan was already defined by hate, his hate of the Indian, before Ethan's journey began. Albert prayed that his own journey would define him not by hate or bitterness, but by the love that animated it, however successfully or unsuccessfully it concluded. He rose and resumed his walk, taking one step at a time into the future, and farther south.

Not long after he broke free of the seas of wildflowers, the prairie became monotonous, mostly flat, but with some sweeping hills, and almost entirely colorless. There were also many sandy washes and occasional small canyons. The washes he negotiated easily, leaping onto their shallow floors, taking a few steps, then heaving himself back up to level ground on the other side. The only real danger here was the wildlife. A couple of times he almost stepped on rattlesnakes resting in a wash's shade. Once he crossed the path of a badger, which quickly angered. It bared its teeth and sliced the air with its long claws. Al considered shooting the damned thing, but had no idea what quality of cuisine it would provide. So he backed away and the badger royally occupied the wide berth presented it. The canyons Al mostly circumnavigated, not needing to go more than a quarter mile out of his way. But a few appeared to stretch on for miles, so Al would descend and ascend their steep faces. He fell going down one. Fortunately, he was only a few feet from the bottom of the canyon. The fall—or, more precisely, the landing—was bone-jarring, but he was unhurt. This provided the most excitement he had in Old Missouri.

Until the day of the buffalo.

❧

Really, the prairies of the near southwest of Old America had never been suited for farming. The Dust Bowl of the 1930s, with its heart in the southwest, demonstrated how fragile were the loose, sandy soils of these prairies. The prairies were semi-arid, and the region stretching from Texas up to the Dakotas had once been designated the Great American Desert. Some years of uncharacteristically high rainfalls attracted settlers in the late nineteenth and early twentieth centuries. Then technologies, particularly irrigation, allowed wheat and corn to be cropped in the Great Desert another few decades. With the Age of the Descent, cheap and steady fuel supplies dwindled and then disappeared. At least as dramatically, irrigation depleted massive underground aquifers such as the Ogallala. The lands were once again no longer suited for heavy human habitation and agriculture.

Some forward-looking (and realistic) thinkers had long suggested that the region be returned to what it was before Euro-Americans entered it. In the Age of the Descent, their suggestions were implemented. The vast area was re-established as a buffalo commons. The buffalo was particularly suited to the semi-arid prairies. It could travel long distances without much water. Its cupped hoof shifted rather than compacted the soil. Cattle compacted the soil and also cropped prairie grass nearly to its roots, while buffalo left the grass unmolested a few inches above ground. All told, buffalo did less grazing damage to the land than did cattle, and the prairies could thrive unendingly beneath the benevolent tread of the giant, humped beasts.

Before Al on his trek first sighted the buffalo, he strode in the vicinity of a prairie dog town. A prairie dog metropolis might be more like it. Al reckoned the "town" covered at least five acres. Every few feet chimneys of soil rose, the mounds gathered at the top of prairie dog burrows. The prairie dogs themselves sat atop the mounds, many reared and resting on their rumps, with their forelegs hanging or crossed as if to politely welcome their guest. Those closest to Al's passage ducked inside their dens. The many at safe distances stayed above board. In general, the dogs raised a moderate fuss, really more chittering and cheeping than barking. Al zigzagged through the town as he might cross a minefield, except that these mines were more charming than alarming.

He was just a few hundred yards beyond the prairie dog village when he topped a rise. What he saw took his breath away. Thousands of buffalo stretched as far ahead, and as far to Al's right and left, as he could see. Al had read about the restored buffalo commons and its inhabitants. A mature bull buffalo weighed a ton. A cow was about half the bull's weight. Herds moved in mammoth wedges, some fifty miles long and twenty-five miles wide at their broadest points. Of course, Al had no idea just how big this herd was, but it then seemed to him oceanic. It rustled and roiled in great brown waves. Hovering over these waves was a haze of insects, and diving in and out the haze were the buffalo birds that followed the herds and feasted on their buggy bounty. Here and there the herd broke into clearings, in which bulls squared off for breeding rights. The giants pawed furiously then charged, their collisions producing sounds like cannon fire and sending fist-sized clumps of hair flying. There was another strong feature to the buffalo: especially in this number they were powerfully rank of odor, so much so that Al was not sure which of his senses was more overwhelmed, that of sight or that of smell.

Then there occurred a disturbance in the herd. If the herd was oceanic, it was as if a great storm brewed out to sea. Russet waves nearest Al surged and began to boil steadily. Gradually a thundering noise from deep in the ocean of buffalo overtook the sounds of the beasts nearer to Al. Next, he saw a huge dust cloud rise in the distance. It rose and folded into itself, then swelled larger and larger. The bulls ceased their fighting and stood at attention. Some cows nervously steered their calves out of the herd.

Al realized something terrible was occurring: a stampede. He panicked. Where could he turn? The stampede was charging on him. He saw no trees or washes nearby. In a scattered, vague way, it dawned on him that the prairie dog town, a few hundred yards behind him, might offer his only chance of survival. He turned and ran for his life.

The roar grew and deafened him. He glanced over his shoulder and saw that the buffalo he had been observing were now galloping behind him. He pushed himself to run even faster. For moments that seemed eternal, the buffalo closed on him. It was not clear he would reach the prairie dog town before they trampled him. He held on to his rifle, but threw aside his backpack and gained speed.

At last he achieved the town and darted among the dirt mounds. He ran the length of a football field inside the town and ducked behind two chimneys situated especially close together. Now he faced the oncoming charge. Every nerve in him pushed and pulled him to jump and run, but he knew a run would be futile. He forced himself to hold his place. Swirling clouds of sand stung his face and dug at his eyes. The buffalo churned almost on him, leaning forward and downward for speed. Then a bull made it inside the town and a foreleg dropped into a prairie dog's hole. The bull brayed terrifyingly. It plowed more than lifted its leg out of the den. Al heard the sickening breaking of bone. The buffalo's leg dangled and swung, almost severed below the knee. Its bowels evacuated themselves in a gush. Buffalo charging from behind hit the beast and knocked him off his feet. The downed bull blocked the path of a pursuing buffalo. Blood and entrails exploded from it as it was crushed by the surge from its rear. Then two more buffalo were going down, and Al realized he might suddenly have shelter.

He ran toward the pile-up, what was now a four-ton boulder of flesh and fur. He lay down and covered his head. The buffalo tumbled, rushed, and blasted around him. He was enveloped by a phantasmagoria of dirt, blood, and shit—a tornado of buffalo and squawking birds and ricocheting bugs. But he was alive.

Finally the storm ended. The last of the herd straggled by, mostly injured animals. Cows nudged along limping calves. Some of the hurt, exhausted, fell and lay snorting, their sides heaving. The thunder of the receding stampede lessened. Al began to return to himself. He felt his legs, held his hands in front of his face. Miraculously, he was alive and whole. His heartbeat slowed. He drew deep breaths. He said, "Thank you, God. God, thank you." Euphoric, he rolled in the dirt and then picked himself up. He steadied himself on his feet and realized he was parched, thirstier than he had ever been.

He turned to watch the receding herd. Heaven knew when it would stop stampeding. He watched for several minutes, until all that remained of the buffalo was the dust in its wake. Then Al had the sensation of eyes on his back. When he turned back around, he faced four horse-mounted Indians, men slightly clad in buffalo fur and leather. One had an arrow still nocked on his bowstring. All looked on him impassively, with little apparent curiosity. Al's curiosity, however, was immediately aroused.

Two of the Indians were clearly of Asian lineage.

16

The horsemen looked down on Albert. His immediate concern was the rider with the nocked bow and arrow. But then the apparent leader called the names of two of his companions. He told them to butcher the fallen buffalo. Al realized these men—along with several others he now saw in the distance—were hunting the buffalo. They meant no harm to him, though they had caused the buffalo stampede.

The leader returned his attention to Al. "My name is He Who Sees Far." He smiled. "Earlier I was known as John Gimbel. And you?"

Al smiled back. "I am and always have been named Albert Simmel. Please call me 'Al.'"

"We are sorry you were in the path of our hunt, Al. Are you all right? It seems the Sacred Spirit has smiled on you."

"I think I am fine," said Al. "More than you would have imagined. And that thanks to the Sacred Spirit, indeed." He paused. "I have lost all my supplies."

"Are you traveling far?"

Al noticed the reticence in the query. The Indian did not ask where he was going, only if he had far yet to go. Here was someone not grasping or insecure or defensive in face of others. He answered: "I am not certain how much farther I have to go. But my journey is surely not over."

"Then allow us, by way of apology, to replenish your provisions. You can return to camp with us. Stay the night. There will be dance and celebration. You are welcome."

So it was that Al met his first real, live meta-Indians. He knew, roughly, what meta-Indians were. They included those of Native American blood who, after the return of the sprawling buffalo commons, reverted to the way of their ancestors. They followed the great herds across the prairies. Like their ancestors, they depended on buffalo meat for food, on buffalo hides for blankets and tipi sidings and clothing, on buffalo sinews for bowstrings and slingshots. So long as the buffalo lasted the meta-Indians' way of life, like the plains on which the buffalo trod, was entirely sustainable.

And this was why their numbers included, ethnically speaking, not only Native Americans, but Euro-Americans, Asian-Americans, African Americans, and others who admired and joined their sustainable existence, living basically in harmony with the earth and its creatures. This existence appeared quite sensible to people of various races after the Age of the Descent, particularly those who were otherwise reduced to poverty anyway. Hence these people were as a whole meta-Indians—not literally ethnic Indians, but people following the *idea* of the plains nomadic Indians as they understood it. Founding meta-Indians were devoted students and theorists of Indian history and anthropology, and realized they could not exactly replicate the conditions of the nineteenth-century Indians, since different conditions now prevailed. Meta-Indians sought to appropriate and implement the Indian way of life under their own, unique conditions of time and place.

"Ride with me," He Who Sees Far said, offering his hand. Al took it and was lifted up behind the buffalo hunter. The horse skittered and pranced nervously, then He Who Sees Far nudged it into a walk, allowing the horse plenty of rein so it could observe and pick its way over the treacherous, prairie-dog-pocked ground. As they reached the edge of the prairie dog town, some of the dogs made their way back above ground. They surveyed the damage around them gingerly, like survivors emerging from bomb shelters after an especially turbulent attack. Al smiled to himself, then gripped He Who Sees Far's sides as the horse jolted and, back on safe ground, broke in a gallop toward the meta-Indian village.

❧

The camp was situated near the bow of a river. Cottonwoods and willows lined the river and provided shade for the tipis under their swaying boughs. The party's arrival occasioned some excitement, all the more so when He Who Sees Far shouted out that the hunt had been successful. Children and dogs ran beside the incoming horses. The children looked at Al with frank curiosity.

Al saw that the village was a mixture of the ancient and the modern. There were the tipis, made from poles and buffalo skins as Indians had built them from time immemorial. But there were also porcelain, iron-claw-footed bathtubs, lined up as water troughs. At the far, open end of the bow, there was a soccer field, with chalk lines in the dirt and large plastic and nylon net goals. Two wagons were backed end to end beneath a dead neon-bulbed sign that read "Alvin's Bar & Grill" and bore a smaller sign below it with the wording "Food Served Cold, Beer Served Warm." Atop the wagons sat planks on barrels—the bar of the Bar and Grill—and behind the planks stood a few patrons, who raised their mugs and toasted the victorious hunters. The mishmash of anachronisms made Al aware, for the first time, that they were riding on hornless English saddles, saddles that, he learned later, had been donated by a member of the tribe related to British aristocracy.

For the remainder of the afternoon, Al settled into the village. An Indian woman fetched blankets and led Al to an unoccupied tent, a kind of guest tipi. She filled him in on details of when they would eat, where he could wash up for dinner, and told him that the men bathed in the river at mornings, the women at evenings. (Here she mischievously wrinkled her nose, hinting that Al's body odor indicated the need for a bath.) Then He Who Sees Far escorted Al around the village, taking him first to the bar for a drink, then introducing him to various dignitaries. They went last to visit the tribe's chief.

The chief was a large, well-built man with long and flowing red hair. He was Chief Sky Rider—so named, Al later learned, because as a youth he was a champion high and long jumper at the Indians' inter-tribal track meets. It was said that he had to restrain himself to keep from shooting and drifting off the earth's surface altogether. But the chief exercised no restraint in greeting Al. He complained that he had too few visitors and that hospitality was one of the great joys of his life. He repeatedly slapped Al on the back and laughed in delight. Then he said they must go to the bar and share a drink. Al was reluctant since the drink was strong and he was already a bit lightheaded from the earlier draught. But Chief Sky Rider insisted, backslapping and guffawing. "I was Jimmy O'Reilly in an earlier life. And one must be true to all of one's heritage." He practically dragged Al back to the bar, where Al thankfully found a milder beverage and the chief presided for hours, grandly inviting passersby to meet their visitor and join him in a toast to the visitor.

Al was very happy before they were done, both because such welcome was lavished on him and for more basic chemical reasons. He and the chief stumbled back to his tipi and Al was glad he had some time to nap before the night's festivities. "O ho!" roared the chief at the door to Al's tent. "There will be more spirits, and spirits of all kinds they'll be, when we gather for dinner. O ho!" With that he applied one last, hearty backslap, which propelled Al inside to his rest.

❧

The village was bustling when Al later emerged from his tipi. Campfires were being lighted in a large circle, with a pole at the very center of the circle. Men, women, and children were laying buffalo blankets inside and outside the circle, and picnic-style arranging settings of cups, plates, bowls, and gleaming cutlery (another gift from the tribesman of aristocratic ancestry). Once everyone had gathered, servers walked about the grounds bearing pots, ladling out drinks of beer and sarsaparilla, with steaming bowls of buffalo stew and plates of beans and buffalo brisket. Bread rolls were introduced with hilarity. The bakers came with hot rolls to the outsides of the circle. Then the children were invited to compete in seeing who could throw rolls the farthest, an arrangement that neatly and naturally resulted in serving all eaters. Those near received rolls from the littlest children, who of course could not throw far, and those more distant snatched from the air bread tossed by the teenagers.

Al sat at a place of honor, with Chief Sky Rider, his strikingly tall and beautiful wife, and the chief's oldest daughter and her husband. For the chief and his party, large rocks were placed and covered with buffalo robes, providing excellently comfortable backrests. The chief again proved good company, drinking and eating with gusto, telling vivid stories and jokes, teasing the grandchildren who now and then ventured in their midst to get parents' permissions to disappear into the woods and to the river, for games of hide-and-seek, swimming, and so forth.

As darkness thickened, more wood was piled on the various campfires, so that the flames leapt five or six feet high and all the celebrants flickered in yellow and orange light. Then singers (there were no drums) started. After a few minutes of singing alone, young men and women began to dance in a circle, moving clockwise. Their faces and bodies were painted red and white. They danced with a sober joy, intense and yet clearly enjoying themselves. Throughout the evening, Chief Sky Rider translated the lyrics that were sung.

Ro'rani, ro'rani. "The snow lies there," said the chief.

Gosi'pa' havi'ginu' "The Milky Way lies there."

Dena' Gayo'n, De' na ga yoni. "A slender antelope, a slender antelope."

Bawa' doro'n, Ba' wa do' roni. "He is wallowing upon the ground."

Pasu' wi'noghan. "The wind stirs the willow."

Wai-va wi'noghan. "The wind stirs the grasses."

Dombi'na so' wina', dombi'na so' wina. "The rocks are ringing, the rocks are ringing."

Through the evening, Sky Rider also explained in depth the meaning of the dance. It was the Ghost Dance, he said, and it went back to a prophet of the late nineteenth and early twentieth centuries. He was a Paiute named Wovoka. His father disappeared when Wovoka was in his teens, and he was adopted by a rancher named David Wilson.

Wovoka was rechristened Jack Wilson. The rancher and his family treated Jack well, and he joined with them in daily prayers and Bible reading. As a young man, Wovoka/Wilson had a religious experience. The sun was eclipsed on January 1, 1889, and Wovoka fell into a trance. He said later that he had been lifted up into heaven and brought before God. In heaven he was anointed a prophet.

Wovaka was said to have possessed miraculous power, especially concerning the control of weather. He transplanted a tree during a fierce rain without getting wet. He lighted his pipe by simply pointing it at the sun. During droughts, he made water appear in empty containers. On a witheringly hot summer day, he produced a huge block of ice on top a blanket.

But Wovoka's teachings were at the center of his prophecy, and would outlive his wonderworks. He taught that God's moral requirements of humanity were threefold and simple, at least in their expression: Do not steal. Do not lie. Do not engage in war. He also taught the people the Ghost Dance, which Al was now witnessing. The circling dance symbolized the ingathering of all the Indian people. Someday God would draw together all Indians, not only those living but those who had died across many centuries, who would be resurrected and returned to the face of the earth. He would return buffalo to the land, from which the white man would disappear. All evil would be swept from the world, so that humanity and animals and nature would live in harmony. The Ghost Dance, then, was a demonstration of faith. It was faith that God was already at work bringing

Wovoka's promises to life. And it was faith for the future, that soon the dead would be resurrected and the earth would be restored to peace and fullness.

At first this fascinating tale struck Al as a fable, if a beautiful one. But when he thought on it for a few minutes, he realized how much Wovoka's prophecy was based on Christian beliefs about resurrection and a new heaven and new earth. Furthermore, he reflected, Wovoka's hopes and expectations were not entirely unreasonable. After all, the buffalo had been restored to the land, and most whites had departed it. He chuckled to himself and allowed that God might well be at work among the meta-Indians, who after all were a people of deep peace and abundant hospitality.

After a few hours of the dancing, Chief Sky Rider had offered all his explanation and fell silent. As the chief and his family joined the circle dance, Al leaned back on a fur-cushioned rock and looked up into the night sky, the cavernous bowl towering above and all around him. The stars burned like campfires spread across a vast black plain. They were as numerous as all the Indians who had died across the centuries, some to old age, some because of the depredations of the white man, some in hunting accidents or lightning strikes or washed away in floods or ruined by hunger. Then Al thought about the majesty of the stars, how they were older and larger than our sun, how they blinked like beacons from the first to the last man or woman of the universe in its unthinkably long history.

After a while, Chief Sky Rider and his family returned to Al's side. They invited him to stay a few days and rest, if he would like, and he said he would like. They promised arrangement of provisions when he did go on his way. They asked him about his own faith and way of life. And so the talk went on late into the night, even as the circle dancers continued, the ranks replenished by youngest to the oldest, including some, said the chief, who had stepped tall in the Ghost Dance for several decades. The talk ebbed and flowed, even as some conversationalists drifted and dozed, then awakened and, once they had gathered what was being discussed, rejoined the talk. But finally the periods of silence grew longer than the periods of conversation, and the chief said whoever wanted was free to go to bed.

Al was at that point where trying to remain awake was a torture. He heard the chief's permission gladly, and walked back to his tent. There he lay and listened to the creek flowing behind his tipi, lapping across rocks and sand. And soon he succumbed to sustained sleep, sleep for the rest of the night.

And when he slept, he dreamed. In his dream he traveled and arrived at a rushing river. It was late, and dark. He stretched out to rest, but suddenly a man appeared above him in the blackness. The man was clad in a hooded robe, and Al could make out nothing of his identity. For some reason the man fell upon him and began to wrestle with him. They tumbled across the sand, grunting and grappling at one another. And then the man seemed to want to quit his wrestling, but Al (quite reasonably, it seemed in the dream) now did not want to stop.

So they wrestled for hours, tumbling back and forth, sometimes rolling in and out of the cold river. Then the man said, "Let me go, for the day is breaking." And Al said, "I will not let you go, unless you bless me." And then the man ceased his struggle, and his hood fell from off his head. Al saw the man's face. The man was his father. The man struck Al sharply on his hip.

There the dream ended.

All next morning, Al's hip was sore. He limped as he moved about the encampment.

17

Al's next scheduled stop for news about Valerie's flight path was a Methodist church in the town of Old Melville, Old Kansas. His new friends, He Who Sees Far and Chief Sky Rider, responded happily when they learned this. The river beside which the meta-Indians camped ran southerly, and would take him most of the way to Old Melville. He Who Sees Far insisted on gifting Al with a wood-hewn canoe, and that afternoon he said his goodbyes and set off from the bustling village.

Soon the river widened and its current strengthened. Al had only occasionally to dip his paddle to keep the canoe straight; otherwise obliging nature did the work. He put down the paddle and lifted his arms, and like an avian keeper releasing doves from his cupped palms, sent prayers aloft. He thought how easy it was to doubt, how likely it was to disbelieve, in a world so full of disappointments and suffering. He thanked God again, for faith and the privilege of gratitude. And he added a prayer for his mother, about whom he had thought too little on this trip. Al's craft rounded one long, sweeping bend and brought him just in sight of a mountainous weeping willow. The willow's branches gracefully bowed, like mint-green fireworks erupting and arcing out of the sky and into the muddy water.

At another point, the river flowed through flatland, with no trees and few bushes growing on its banks. Then Al had the uncanny sensation that the river had stopped moving, while abandoned farmhouses and barns and silos started drifting by on each side of him. He could blink and momentarily regain the right, actual visual perspective, but soon the optical illusion reasserted itself and he seemed again to be stationary, watching the wide, usually still and anchored world roll by. He waved at meta-Indian children who ran riverside to greet him, and halloed at the occasional grazing buffalo. Eventually he was carried out of buffalo country and beyond meta-Indian camps.

It grew dark, but Al was not tired—he was not working hard. He elected to keep moving into the night. Again, as it had in the meta-Indian camp, the starry sky yawned open above him. It was as if he had proceeded into some stupendously large cavern. But now he thought of the shimmering stars not so much as campfires as galactic lighthouses, or the lanterns of anxious families holding vigil, awaiting the return of loved ones from distant seas. He fancied Val holding one such lantern, probing into the dark with eager hopefulness. He found that he could execute lilting double-strokes of the paddle and set the canoe revolving gently. Then the stars and their constellations gamboled around him, above in the sky and below in their watery reflections. He rode a gigantic and all-encompassing merry-go-round. And he had only to dip and twist his paddle to straighten the canoe and resume his ordinary course. In his enchantment, he forgot his worries and forgot the time. Suddenly, though he could hardly believe it, the sun was rising over the river's left bank, setting the currents aglitter, a curving field of diamonds free for the taking. He felt his tiredness and cast ashore, where he built a small fire and fried some beans and bread. He ate. Then he lay down for a nap.

❧

Al awoke to a racket of gobbling and squawking. He opened his eyes to a sight. Four rafts, each about fifteen feet long, were tied together. The three trailing rafts were caged with chicken wire and laden with cargo of what he would later learn were no fewer than two hundred turkeys. Turkey feathers and hay straw littered the breeze. On the lead raft stood a tent and cooking kettle, along with a woman, a white-haired, scrawny man, and three yipping hounds. The man called out, "Ahoy, matey. Permission to come ashore." He waved a wooden right hand, painted fire-engine red. The thumb and all but the middle finger were broken and gone, and Al witnessed the incongruous sight of what looked like someone flipping him off.

"Your finger, Billy," said the wife.

"Sorry," he said, self-consciously lowering the wooden appendage. "I just smashed my hand. I forget that waving it in its present condition does not give the appearance of an amiable greeting." He cackled.

Al welcomed the marine train ashore, and there greeted William Reziff and his wife, Jane. The man may have been scrawny, but he was as spry as a banty rooster and leapt from his raft onto dry ground. He made his introductions and busily set about tying off his noisy vehicle to shoreside trees. Finished with his chores, he offered Al a cigar. The two men lit up, while Jane disappeared into the riverside forest, saying she had seen some apple trees and was in mind of some dessert with supper.

Al and William smoked and got acquainted. Reziff explained that he and his wife were taking the turkeys to market. They had left their farm under the able management of their sons and twin daughters, and would be on their trip two weeks, to and from market. He related how much the couple loved the trips to market, where they would earn a sizeable, fresh intake of cash, and enjoy a night out on the town. Then they would spend a day or two shopping. The boys needed some new boots and dungarees, the twins were in need of dresses and presents for their soon-arriving birthday. William also planned to pick up a straw gardener's hat for Jane. "But don't mention it to her," he interjected. "It's a surprise."

Al in turn outlined his mission to pick up Valerie, and told how he had been traveling for two months. He provided no details about the circumstances that had separated them, but simply said she was visiting with friends. He said his journey was near its end, which he assumed or at least vigorously wished to be the case. William was fascinated that Al had traveled so far, and asked about high points on the way. Al mentioned the buffalo stampede and his sojourn with the meta-Indians. That suggested to William an account of his own pleasant relations with the metas. Al talked about witnessing the Ghost Dance, and William expressed envy that he had never had the privilege.

After awhile Jane reappeared, bearing a basket filled with green apples. "Ask him to dinner, Billy," she said.

William smiled. "Help me feed the turkeys and we'll treat you to dinner."

William handed Al a bucket of feed and showed him how to open the cage doors, then the men wandered about the milling, jumping turkeys, casting grain. The turkeys slowed and quieted their gobbling at the pleasure of repast, till their noise stilled to a melodious clucking sound. Once the buckets were empty of feed, the men dipped them in the river and replenished water troughs on the turkeys' rafts.

All the while the dappled dogs capered about the campsite. They admonished the turkeys with rounds of barking and chased squirrels into trees. The treed squirrels wielded their thinned tails and snapped them like whips, taunting the dogs. Jane had busied herself slicing and sugaring apples, mixed dough, then poured the concoction into an iron pot, which she buried under the smoldering coals of a fire. Soon the three sat down to a sumptuous feast of turkey, bacon-greased green beans, and wheat toast. There was plenteous red wine. Then Jane dug the pot out of the coals, and presented the most delicious apple cobbler Al had ever eaten. They ate and drank and talked. When they were too full to countenance one more bite, all three carried plates and cups to the riverside and washed the dishes. They resuscitated the fire to a full blaze. Jane lighted a pipe and William produced more cigars for himself and Al.

As is the way with shared food and drink, the couple and Al began to feel comfortable, even friendly. They soon fell to telling stories, and so Al learned how William Reziff had lost his right hand.

Reziff grew up in eastern Old Oklahoma, where one of the pastimes was a curious custom called noodling. This entailed men (and women) descending into rivers, where they would locate sunken logs, junked automobiles, or sinkholes where catfish were hiding. The intrepid fishermen would then poke and prod—noodle—in these tangled, murky environs. When they touched a catfish (and hopefully not a water moccasin instead) they would jam their hand or a hay hook into its maw, and wrestle it out of the water. This was easy enough with small fish, but expert noodlers went after bigger game. Some catfish were mammoth, weighing sixty or seventy pounds, and it was never a sure thing that even the strongest, most adept noodler would land such monsters.

Anyhow, William was an avid noodler. He preferred to use a hay hook rather than his bare hand, as did most noodlers who went after the big fish. They would tie a rope to the hay hook on one end and their wrist on the other. This arrangement assured that the noodler could remain attached to the fish while standing up out of the water, where they could keep their breath and engage in prolonged battles.

William did not like ropes. They could break, and when they were soaked they swelled and could uncomfortably tighten on the wrist. William preferred steel cable, wrapped around his gloved wrist, as his noodling leash. It was foolhardy, perhaps, but he was young and supposed himself immortal. His cable never broke, and his biggest catch was a fifty-five-pounder he had fought for two hours before he finally dragged it ashore. The experience was so euphoric that he was confirmed in his methods and said he would never go back to rope.

One fine day William went to the river and noodled along a bank until he felt an overhang, beneath which seemed to be a fairly good-sized cave. William took a deep breath, submerged, and swam into the cave. He groped about the sides until he felt the tense skin and tendril-whiskers of a catfish. He swept his hand in search of the animal's snout, and realized this was a very large fish indeed. He thrashed and jammed the fish between himself and the cave wall, then thrust his hay hook into fish's mouth. Immediately the fish responded with flopping and jerking. William found the river bottom and set his feet, then plowed backward with the fish in tow. He thought the beast was going to yank his shoulder out of joint, but he attained the cave's mouth, found waterlogged tree limbs to grasp with his free hand, and pulled the fish out into the river proper.

In the open river the fish took off, jerking William off his feet. He kept his nose above water as the fish towed him. This was not too big a problem in the relatively shallow water, which kept the fish from going deep and pulling William under. At intervals the fish would tire and William would regain his feet, set his heels in the gravelly bottom, and apply tension to keep the fish from resting. Eventually William would tire a bit and the fish would again surge forward. This back-and-forth struggle went on for at least two hours—William could tell by the sun's changed position in the sky. Finally the beast wrapped and lodged the cable in the forking branches of a submerged tree. The fish would not let William pull him out of the forks and onto the riverbank. William would not allow the fish to pull him through the forks, which anyhow were too narrowly close together for William's passage. In stalemate, fish and fisherman jerked at one another for an hour or more. Then it began to rain. At first lightly, but then heavily, so much so that William could barely see through the sheets of rain to the river's bank. It rained for at least an hour, and kept on raining. William realized the river was rising.

When the river rose to his neck, he finally, in desperation, decided to abandon the fish. But every time he pulled the cable back for free play, to release his wrist, the fish pulled back its direction, tautening the steel around the swollen wrist. Still the rain fell. The river lapped at William's chin. Now he drew the bowie knife strapped to his belt and began to hack at one fork on the tree, to release himself and the fish from their entrapment in the fork. But the branch was thick and waterlogged, and he made slow progress. He would never get it hacked apart before the water covered his head.

The water rose now above his lips, and every time he sucked air through his nostrils he would draw water into his nose. Coughing, near to drowning, he realized he had one last chance. He applied the knife to his wrist, and found it so numb that he could start the sawing on his own flesh.

Here Jane and Al confessed that they could not stand to hear the rest of the story in any detail.

"Anyway," William said, and paused to relight his cigar. "I got the hand off, and crawled out of the water. I wrapped my belt around the stump as tight as I could, and went to find help." He paused again.

Behind an exhaled cloud of blue cigar smoke, he said, "The damned fish got away. Once in awhile they say noodlers will still come across a big cat dragging steel cable. They leave it alone. It won't take another hand, or a life."

❧

After this gruesome tale, Al thought he would nudge them into less intense storytelling territory. He asked how Jane and William met. Now the couple chuckled and exchanged knowing looks.

"Let me tell this one, Billy," said Jane. William shook his head.

Jane said that some years after William lost his hand, but was still young, hard times descended on folks in eastern Old Oklahoma. William's father had died, and one winter his mother took sick. William had three younger siblings, and the whole family was starving. So William broke into a bakery and stole five loaves of bread. He was apprehended on his way out. As is too often the case in hard times, the law had turned especially draconian and William was sentenced to five years in prison—one year for every loaf.

After William had been jailed two years, hating every minute, a drunken guard one night left the key in William's cell door. William sneaked out of the jail and took flight. He ran through the night and, as the sun started to rise, took refuge in a grubby, bushy ditch on the outskirts of a town. He planned to hide there through the day, then resume his escape in the dark. But along about mid-day, he heard cries from a farm near the ditch. He peeked out to see a barn on fire. A woman was standing outside the blazing barn. "My Tommy's in there!" she screamed. She was a widow and her two boys were all she had. Tommy's younger brother tried to rush into the barn, but the widow would not let him go. William's instinct was to run and help, but he knew he would be caught and returned to captivity if he did so. He waited another five minutes, thinking, praying some help would come. But none did. The terrible cries continued. He could stand it no longer, and knew he would not be able to stand himself if he passively watched while a child burned. So William sprinted to the barn and inside it. The smoke was almost blinding, the heat terrible, but he saw the teenaged boy crouched, paralyzed in a corner. He and the boy were separated by a barrier of hellishly hot flame.

William ran back outside, crying for an axe. The woman dashed to a woodpile and returned with the axe. William rounded the barn to stand outside where the boy was crouched. He yelled at the boy to edge away from the wall, then he swung at the wall clumsily, with one hand. Fortunately the wood was old and thin, and William broke through and snatched the boy out of the barn just as the hayloft collapsed to the floor where the boy had been.

Then, ironically, cruelly, the town's police and firemen arrived on the scene. The word had gotten out about a one-handed jailbreaker, and the police rearrested William as the firemen hosed water on the leaning skeleton of the already ruined barn.

The widow said she owed the one-handed man everything, and she never missed a weekly visit to him while he served out the remainder of his sentence (not shortened, but not lengthened, either, because of his good deed). Over three years of these visits the widow and William fell in love.

"I was that widow," Jane said. "And two days after William got out of prison, we were married."

William said, "Ain't never looked back, either, have we, honey?"

Jane squeezed her husband by the arm and laid her head on his shoulder. "We have not, Billy, we have not. Mr. Simmel, we have our two boys and we have twins from our own union. And maybe you have already noticed, but we are content. Sometimes times are hard, but we are merry, altogether we are. How can you not be, a family gathered around a man like Billy Reziff, who two or three times over has seen the worst life can offer, and has decided he can live with it?" With that she slapped William on the rump, and addressed him, "But enough with glorying you, old man. We've still got chores to do before we sleep."

They busied about extinguishing the campfire and unfurling bedrolls. Al watched the pleasant, companionable puttering, and finished his cigar. Then everyone said good night, and every one of them rested well that night.

18

Al traveled with the Reziffs another four days down the river, and from there it was a day's hike to Old Melville. He found the pastor of the Methodist Church in Old Melville, and learned that Valerie and her escort had passed through some years before. Al's heart lifted each time he got news of Val, and knew that she had made it at least that far in her journey, and that her trail had not run cold for him. The pastor informed him that the next staging point in Val's flight was at the Bremen Street Episcopal Church, in Old Kansas City.

Five days later, Al entered Old Kansas City. The city was hopping, abustle with the annual celebration of its Great Buffalo Barbeque Festival. The festival drew thousands from surrounding areas, not least because of the excellent food. It also attracted a diversity of religious people, some of whom scheduled their church denomination's annual convention to coincide with the barbeque bash.

In the fissiparous ways of Protestant Christianity, a host of religious hybrids had emerged in the Old US since the middle of the twenty-first century. Extremist fundamentalist Christians, long theocratic at heart, had allied with extremist fundamentalist Muslims and formed the Jesus Jihadists. Now most popular in the Deep South, Jesus Jihadists clad their females in burkhas and focused on the Jesus of the book of Revelation, whom they depicted as sword-wielding and eager to spill mega-gallons of blood. Meanwhile the High Desert Rastafarians, situated in the Joshua Tree–dotted, sparsely populated regions north of Old Palm Springs, had found a territory in which they could partake of ritual ganja without legal molestation.

There were also Buddhist Mennonites and Lutheran Unitarians. But perhaps the religious group that had grown the fastest in the Age of the Descent was Mormonism and its various offspring. Old Salt Lake City burgeoned into a city of three million and was renamed Mormonopolis. Among other developments, conservative evangelicals merged with conservative Mormons and formed the Evangelical Church of Latter-Day Saints. (In all this ferment, liturgical churches such as Al's Episcopal denomination—along with certain Roman Catholic, Lutheran, and Reformed traditions—still relied on the worship forms and content rooted as early as the second century, and were among those who had maintained the highest degree of Christian orthodoxy.)

Al ventured into the city's downtown, where both the Bremen Street Episcopal Church and the heart of the buffalo festival were located. Passing beneath a dying maple, he kicked aside huge, dried leaves that were brown and crumpled like paper bags. He rounded the corner and came across the carnival. Children ran by with corn dogs and leaning towers of pink cotton candy. Mothers and fathers pursued, issuing a stream of perennial parental warnings: "Don't fall on that stick and choke yourself" and "If you drop that food you're not getting more." A Ferris wheel turned jerkily, propelled by a gear-system attached to a harnessed circle of plodding mules. A steam-powered roller coaster rattled over its track.

Not all was hilarity, however. Al noticed a train of people flowing into and congregating in a park across the street from the Ferris wheel. He decided to investigate. The park's crowd was forming around a central gazebo, on which stood two lecterns.

Al asked a woman standing next to him what was about to happen. She breathlessly informed him that a leading Evangelical Church of Latter-Day Saints prophet was about to speak at a spiritual forum. The prophet was Virgil Thurston, the author of bestselling books on strict childrearing and the central role of America in Christianity. The spiritual forum was a regular event in which religious leaders held forth on their faiths. They stood at one podium and gave ten-minute expositions on their primary beliefs. Then anyone who wanted to rebut or question or affirm the speaker was invited to speak at the second podium. Next the lead speaker would reply, and so the dialogue rocked back and forth for up to three hours.

The woman had just finished her explanation when a man of medium height, built like a wrestler, appeared on the gazebo's platform. Murmurs of excitement like static electricity crackled through the crowd. Virgil Thurston, wiping sweat off his brow beneath blond hair, waved and delightedly pointed his finger at particular supporters. Camera shutters clicked. Thurston turned his left and most photogenic profile toward busy press photographers. An introduction of Thurston as "perhaps the leading spokesperson for evangelical Mormons everywhere" followed. Then Thurston occupied one of the podiums.

"Friends, neighbors, supporters—and detractors . . ." Here he winked. "Welcome to this forum. I am privileged and delighted to visit with you this afternoon. I want to talk with you about the Evangelical Church of Latter-Day Saints: what we believe, what we stand for, and how we believe we increase the greatness of this already great nation, the Old United States of America.

"Many, many years ago, thousands of years ago, as the Bible attests, certain tribes of Israel disappeared. For centuries people wondered and puzzled over where they went, what happened to them. Then in the nineteenth century it was revealed to the prophet Joseph Smith where they went, and how even in ancient times America played a key role in God's plans. They came here, to what would become the USA. They wandered and practiced the faith of an earlier famous exile, Israel's prophet Moses, and eventually their descendants settled in the wilds of what we now know as the great state of Old Utah."

Here there were smatterings of applause. Al was disturbed by what seemed to him such a clear departure from classical Christianity. Israel, not Old America or any other state, was God's chosen nation. Old America had no uniquely superior role to play in the salvation of the world. Then the spectators quickly silenced themselves.

"As most or all of you know, Joseph Smith and his brave followers went on to establish the Mormon faith, overcoming the great odds of the desert wilderness, hostile Indians, and even more hostile whites, or Gentiles. These earliest Mormons discovered ancient documents and received fresh visions from God. For decades they were persecuted, scorned, treated worse than the dirt that they farmed. But truth prevails, and here truth prevailed so that the Church of the Latter-Day Saints prospered and grew. And grew. And grew. And today Mormonism is a leading religion in America and, more and more, across other parts of the world.

"It so happened—mainly because of bigotry and misunderstandings—that the most vigorous opponents of Mormons were, for a century or more, evangelical Christians. The evangelicals did not see that we, too, are Christians. They did not appreciate that we, too, understand the Old United States as playing a crucial role in God's plan to bring to completion his work for the world and its salvation. They did not see for a while—and thank God that is now behind us—they did not see how we added to their faith only to deepen and grow it and fit it for these latter days.

"Now I represent the millions of those who are today both evangelical and Mormon. Together . . ." He paused for rhetorical effect. "Together"—and here he raised his voice and shot a finger heavenward—"together in this age we now serve God . . ." The sought-for applause came, crescendoing and ceasing only when Thurston smiled and raised his palms for silence.

"How do we serve God? First, we recognize that God's most important institution on the face of the earth is family. We love children. We birth many children and we rear them in God's ways. They learn that their fathers are the leaders of the family, the mothers followers to their faithful husbands, and that both are to be obeyed and honored by their children. All this we know from the Bible and its prophets.

All this we know from the Bible and its prophets? Al thought. *Really? Must women be subordinate to men? And is the family, rather than the church, God's most important institution on the face of the earth?*

"We are also true patriots. We know that the family has been made free, and been made paramount, in the land Old America, which God has given us the privilege of loving and serving. As no other place in the world, no other place in history, America is the country where fathers can most truly be fathers, mothers can most truly be mothers, and children can truly be children of God.

"It is our destiny, our most precious, God-given destiny, to carry the faith of Jesus Christ and his great work for the family to the ends of the earth. And someday, we hope, we pray, we *know*, we will carry that mission beyond the earth and throughout the universe. Our faith is vast and glorious. And we are the carriers of that faith not just to this planet, but to all planets. The families we build here and now will one day become kings and queens and princes on all planets, planets in this solar system and beyond!

Many members of the audience were again excited and expressive. Whistles sounded along with handclaps and hearty exclamations. There were also a few catcalls and boos, from spectators who disagreed with the speaker. Al stayed quiet, but was beginning to think he should speak once the opportunity was available.

"Let us, then, thank God. We thank God for showing us the way of salvation. We thank God for the family. We thank God for our great Mormon-American mission, and the exciting, gratifying, challenging privilege of serving that mission. We thank God for today, and the blessings we already know. And we thank God for tomorrow, when all the universe will know the blessings of family and of America. Join with me in God's wonderful, amazing work. Join with me, missionaries to all the earth! Join with me, and become missionaries to the stars!"

Thurston then stepped back from the podium and soaked in the audience's approval. He moved to the gazebo's edge and shook hands with enthusiastic supporters. Cameras again clicked and hissed, blinking their insect eyes. Thurston waved expansively. Finally Thurston's introducer, the coordinator of the forum, stepped up behind Thurston's podium.

"We now invite and welcome your responses," he said. "Please confine your remarks to no more than ten minutes, since many may want to have a word."

The crowd simmered, still coming down from its high. There were a few calls to hear more, immediately, from Thurston. The coordinator addressed these, "No. No. We will hear more from Reverend Thurston. As you know, he will have opportunity to respond to each of his responders. Do we have a first response?" Al was gathering his nerve. He waited. "I know it's hard to be the first," the coordinator said. "But come ahead. Surely some of you are anxious to speak, to question, to add to Virgil Thurston's words . . ."

All right, then, Al considered. *Do this on behalf of your own faith. Don't be afraid.* In former times, he would have heard a talk like Thurston's and silently disagreed. But the trials and adventures of his travels made him more audacious, braver. His journey had already made him a different man. He raised his hand and stepped forward. The coordinator approved and beckoned Al onto the platform. He situated Al behind the second podium, flicked a finger at the microphone to make sure it was alive. He asked for a name and then turned back to the audience. "Ladies and gentleman, our first respondent is Mr. Albert Simmel. Please welcome him and give him your full attention."

Al swallowed, took a breath, and launched out.

"Friends, I speak to you today as a fellow Christian. With you, I believe God created the heavens and the earth and all that is in them. With you, I believe Jesus Christ is our true and final redeemer. With you, I believe the Holy Spirit moves in God's people and enlivens that people, the church."

His auditors were still taking stock of the respondent. But these opening words sounded promising, and the crowd offered up applause and a few "amens." Al resumed.

"I commend Virgil Thurston, and I commend the Evangelical Church of Latter-Day Saints, for their enthusiasm. But sometimes, in our enthusiasm, we get a little carried away. We can get our priorities a bit out of order."

Like troubled water, unease burbled and spread through the crowd.

"In the spirit of recognizing that that can happen to any of us, I ask us to reconsider. It is not the family, or Old America, that God has anointed as the most important institution for carrying forth his work on earth. It is the church, the church born of the apostles of the New Testament. In Matthew's Gospel, it is first and foremost the church, not the family or America, to which Jesus assigns the Great Commission to make disciples of all the nations. Throughout the Gospels, Jesus indicates that his followers are his true brothers and sisters, his most important family. And in his Letter to the Ephesians, the Apostle Paul says that it is the church—again, not the family or any nation-state—which is Christ's body in all its fullness.

"The church catholic or universal—spread and spreading over the whole face of the earth—this in Jesus Christ is now God's first family. And the church is God's politics, God's assembly of people and their rightly ordered loyalties."

Uncertain hoots and boos sounded. Al seemed to be saying something different than Thurston, but he was still using much of Thurston's language. The audience grappled with what this meant.

"Now, please hear me. I am not saying Jesus meant to eliminate the family. It's clear that Jesus adored children. He hated divorce. He loved and respected his mother. What I am saying is that Jesus rearranged our loyalties. We are to be loyal to our families, to our country, but we are to be loyal first and above all to the kingdom of God, the kingdom of God revealed in Israel and in Jesus Christ. In the short time I have to speak, let me ask you to think about one thing. Think about your baptism. You, we, have been baptized into the body of Jesus Christ. And our baptisms were declarations of loyalty, loyalty first and last to Jesus Christ and the kingdom he inaugurated and will one day bring to its fullness. Paul says nothing is more basic than baptism. He says being slave or free is not more basic. He says being male or female is not more basic. He says being Jewish or the member of any nation is not more basic. For those of us who have been baptized in Christ, and I know that includes many of you, our root, our true, our most fundamental identity and loyalty has been named. And that is an identity and loyalty rooted in Christ, Christ alone."

There was some more murmuring, but quieter. Al was giving these people something to think about.

"If that is so, we cannot say that our family, our kinship is the most important thing about us. It is important, but it is not more important than our baptism. The water of baptism is thicker than the blood of kinship. And we cannot say that being American is the most important thing about us. It is important that we are Americans, but we belong first and foremost to another polity, the polity of the apostolic church. Our founding document is not the Constitution of the United States but the Bible.

"So I ask you, when you wonder who you are, to think on your baptism. When you sort out your deepest loyalties, think on your baptism. And when you ask what social bodies, what polities, point first and foremost to the gospel and the kingdom of God, think on your baptism.

"Thank you for your gracious attention."

For a few seconds the assembly seemed flabbergasted. But then the moderator gathered his thoughts and stepped to a podium.

"We hear now, and again, from the Reverend Virgil Thurston."

Thurston resumed a microphone, cleared his throat. "Mr. Simmel," he said, "thank you for your thoughts. I must ask, are you saying that Jesus came to pit mother against son, father against daughter? That Jesus came to destroy the family? If so, sir, I say you speak falsely of my Jesus. And if you speak so, sir, I must say further: Unhand my Jesus!"

With this the audience caught glimpses of surer, more familiar ground, and applause broke out.

"Mr. Simmel?" the moderator turned to Al.

"I repeat what I said," Al spoke. "Jesus did not come to destroy the family. He did come, among other things, to move it from the very center of our lives. And he himself said that his call might at times, and unfortunately, pit family members against one another—in the very language you have used, Mr. Thurston, father and mother against son, brother against brother . . ."

Thurston harrumphed. And went in for the kill: "I ask you further, sir, are you an American? Are you a patriot? Or do you use my Jesus as the refuge of a scoundrel, a man disloyal to his country? If so," and now he practically shouted, "I say again: UNHAND MY JESUS!"

Al waited for quiet from the aroused crowd. "I say, Reverend Thurston, that the Christian's highest allegiance is not to his or her country, but to the kingdom of God. The Christian can be a patriot, but in exactly the same way he or she is a good son or daughter. I love my father and mother, and I respect them as indeed my only and most favorite parents. But my love of my parents, like my love of my country, is not exclusive. So I happily allow and endorse your favoritism of your own parents, your own country. But only so, that is, nonexclusively, allowing to all their *conditional* allegiance to their parents, their flag."

The crowd, mostly gathered for Thurston and his message, was set back a bit, once more stalled by some confusion. But it was also resentful that it was once again getting shoved off customary, comfortable, familiar ground. Al realized his complications of the debate were losing him whatever unsteady support he had gained.

"But let me add something, Reverend Thurston, a point of clarification that I think we can all agree on. It is not a matter of 'your Jesus' or 'my Jesus.' If Jesus is Lord, he is Lord of all and not just of you or me. If Jesus is Lord, he is not in my hands or your hands—rather, it is you or I or us who are in his hands."

Thurston put aside all aplomb and apparent civility. Now he spoke directly to the crowd. "Ladies and gentleman, I am not sure what we should make of all this man has said. But I am sure he is a stranger. He is a stranger speaking a strange gospel, a gospel I did not learn at the feet of my parents, a gospel surely foreign to the founding fathers of this great land. With whom will you stand? Will you stand with the faith of your father and the fathers of this country? Or will you stand with a stranger and his strange gospel?"

The crowd mumbled. A few here and there kept their hands at their sides, pondering. But the majority reasserted its confidence, its long-possessed prejudice, and in a building roar demonstrated its approval of Thurston and Thurston's message.

Al left the platform and filtered through the crowd, with most giving him the wide berth of a contagious leper. He ducked his head, muttered politenesses to those clearing his way. And he thought, for the first time, on the innate weirdness of religion, any religion. After all, a robust religion looked on the world not only as it was, but as it *ought to be*, and so it was constantly, unavoidably running against the expectations of those encountering it. But how odd, Al mused, how odd that now, as was true in its beginnings, biblical, apostolic, orthodox Christianity should be regarded as the weirdest and least familiar of all faiths. If God is someone, something radically other than humanity, maybe this in itself testified to the truth of the classical faith.

But for now Al was hungry, and needed to leave this company while it remained harmless, if not exactly friendly, to him. He caught the eye of one woman who seemed to want to talk with him. She had just finished working a hand-pump, and was drinking water out of a tin cup, the liquid making her lips glisten. She did not advance to him, however, and this he understood. He waved, a small, inconspicuous gesture, and departed the fairgrounds.

19

The next station on Al's journey was Omega, located in the Flint Hills of northern Kansas. There he was to find one Reba Wilding, a member of the little city's Catholic Church, for news on where Valerie had gone after departing Omega.

The Flint Hills in early fall were beautiful, green and rolling, dotted with wildflowers and strewn with rutted cattle trails. There were many ponds and small lakes sparkling under the sprawling sky. The hills were not steep, and the travel was effortless. Al followed signs off old Interstate 35 pointing him toward Omega and its twin city, Alpha.

Omega, as it turned out, was a hilltop city. Alpha rested in the valley below it. Locating Omega's Catholic Church, Al talked with a secretary at her desk and was disappointed to learn Reba Wilding was out of town, and would be for several more days. But the plump, white-headed secretary, Joy Yancey, was extraordinarily hospitable. She insisted that Al join her and her husband Donald for dinner.

In the interim before dinner Al secured a hotel room and enjoyed his first hot shower in weeks. He luxuriated in the copious supply of soap, which allowed him to rub all the accumulated grease and dirt off his face and body. He took pleasure watching the dirtied water course off his body and run in muddy rivulets into the drain. For once he violated his usual ethic of conservation, and lingered in the shower for fifteen minutes. He leaned against the wall and let the hot water caress and massage his tired limbs. He washed his hair three times. Finally he finished and the bathroom seethed gently with steam. He dried himself lightly, lowered the toilet lid, and sat in the impromptu sauna until the steam dissipated. Then he dried himself thoroughly and dressed in fresh clothes.

Dinner was sumptuous. It began with dusky purple grapes and rich cheese, accompanied by a full-bodied dark and creamy beer. Then there were hot rolls slathered in cinnamon butter. For the main course the Yanceys prepared chicken-fried steak, garlic mashed potatoes, and bacon-laden green beans—with, of course, more beer. The meal was crowned with a dessert of cherries Donald had picked that very afternoon, chased by a glass of ice cold, fresh milk. The conversation was as outstanding as the food was delicious. The Yanceys were proud of their hometown and delighted in giving Al a crash course on the history of the twin towns, the "Comp Cities," as locals called them.

Not long into the Age of the Descent, the municipalities of Alpha and Omega were founded by visionaries who fled the desolation and confusion of Old Kansas City. The founders believed that wastefulness and competitiveness had ruined the world as they had known it. What, they wondered, if communities were based on harmony and complementarity, rather than strife and divisions? What if two communities were formed to aid one another out of each other's strengths, rather than exploit each other's weaknesses?

In the disillusionment of the oncoming Age of the Descent, the founders did not have trouble finding followers—many from churches and synagogues and mosques who had deeply held ideals but no hope for their realization in Old Kansas City. So a place was found in the Flint Hills. Alpha was built in the valley, Omega on the hilltop overlooking the valley. On the hillsides breweries were built. In the rich loam of the bottoms wheat was cultivated. Thus one city provided beer, the other bread.

Alphaites raised poultry and dairy cattle; Omegans grazed beef cattle in their pastures and on their green winter wheat. Alpha manufactured paper; Omega, ink. The valley town honored shade and darkness, and perfected the growing of healing mushrooms and herbs. The hilltop town venerated light and excelled with master opticians. The valley city specialized in busy activism, the hill city in studious contemplation.

And on it went. Alphaites sought mates among Omegans, and vice-versa. Alphaites excelled in instrumental music, and Omegans in song. The citizens called their philosophy and way of life complementarianism—thus the Comp Cities, for there can be no beginning (Alpha) without an ending (Omega), and no end without a beginning.

Al was enthralled and, despite his impatience to find Valerie, looked forward to exploring the Comp Cities during the waiting period forced on him by Reba Wilding's absence. The Yanceys informed him that there was no better time to experience the Comp Cities and its ways than now. It was fall, and festival season, after all—just as Al had seen at the fair in Thurstonville, where Al had heard the Mormon speech. That very week, in the days he would be awaiting Wilding's return, the Great Feast of Complementarity was under way.

The rich conversation kept Al at the Yanceys' table until after midnight. Then they insisted that he skip the hotel and sleep in their guest room. He started to demur, but the promise of breakfast the next morning was a clincher—he would be a fool to turn down another meal with the Yanceys. After breakfast they would host Al to the second day of the Great Feast.

The guest room was just down the hall from the Yanceys' bedroom. It was sparely appointed, but enlivened by many-colored quilts hanging on two walls. Tired from a day's journey, and ready to doze after beer and the heavy helping of carbohydrates, Al crawled into bed with relish. Before he fell asleep, though, both the Yanceys were snoring. They were a virtuoso duet of nighttime song. While Donald churned in the lower registers and occasionally snorted in punctuated chirrups, Joy emitted more delicate steam-valve sounds and whistled with sustained glissandos. The sounds reminded Al of birdsongs, of rustling leaves and creaking branches and distant rumbling thunder. It was as if he were lying outside, but without any threat of inclement weather or molestation from bandits or a mountain lion or a rabid badger. He dug in contentedly under the covers, and listened till he heard no more and entered the world of dreams.

❧

After breakfast the Yanceys guided Al to the fairgrounds of the Great Feast. The grounds were in some ways like those he'd seen some days ago in Old Kansas City. There was a mule-powered Ferris wheel here, too, as well as cotton candy. There were familiar carnival games such as the ring toss and the floating duck shoot. And there were glass blowers and horseshoe contests.

But there were several pastimes unique to the Comp Cities fair. Barefooted toddlers were lifted into shallow vats of grapes and allowed to stamp to their hearts' content, until their lower legs were dyed deep purple and grape juice dotted their faces. There was an interesting variation on the greased pig chase. Here teenagers were strapped into harnesses and lifted by guy wires, with teammates leveraging them over a three-foot wall and above the squealing pigs. The challenge was to grasp a hog, then hold onto it until you could be maneuvered back over the wall and had deposited the pig in the winner's corral.

There was a wheat-threshing competition, with golden chaff flying and covering the men and women who maniacally gathered sheafs, pounded out grain, and sifted grain from chaff. Al's enjoyment of this event was enhanced by the fact that his new friends, the Yanceys, entered it. Donald laughed throughout, throwing sheaves in Joy's direction, and thereby demonstrated how his face was lined like a road map from decades of exuberant hilarity. At one point he laughed so hard he sucked in a load of straw bits, whereupon the contest was briefly stopped so that Joy could make sure her husband didn't choke to death. Thereafter Donald was ribbed as "The Choker" and seemed to enjoy the joke more than anyone else did.

Throughout the day the Yanceys repeatedly tried to enlist Al in one game or another. Finally he relented, and chose the Mill Wheel Ride. In this event, contestants were strapped to the struts of a steam-powered mill wheel. A barber pole was attached on top of the wheel, and after six contestants were secured on the wheel, it began its turns while onlookers robustly counted revolutions. After he had already agreed to give it a go, Al almost backed out when one of the contestants in the group just before his vomited a sluice of white liquid as he whirled on the wheel. But at that juncture the Yanceys were determined, and Al knew he had a strong stomach (though he could hardly bear the thought of losing any of the wonderful food he had eaten for his last two meals). Much to Al's surprise, the other competitors in Al's group all signaled surrender before he did. He won his round by enduring sixty-three rapid rotations of the wheel. Released from the ride, he was queasy and doubted he would have much supper that evening . . . but he had not lost his previous meals. And he walked away with a prize of four loaves of French bread, which he happily presented to his beaming benefactors.

❧

As excellent as all these events were, the pinnacle of the games of the Great Feast of Complementarity began that evening. Then, and for three following evenings, Alphaites would play against (or rather with) Omegans in an extended basketball game. Now the citizenry of both towns gathered in a vast gymnasium. After weeks of practices, two squads of five players, with five reserves, were ready to square off. Each team included women as well as men, girls as well as boys, from the minimum age of fourteen up to one Alphaite sharpshooter who was fifty-five years old, and an Omegan master ballhandler who would not reveal her age but was reputed to be pushing seventy.

Here Al learned that the complementarians' idea of equality was more nuanced than he had guessed. It did not, after all, exclude competition. Instead, the competition would work toward a peak attained with severe difficulty, balancing and trading players on and off the court for three or four hours each night, working toward an exquisite draw, the "tie that binds," as the Yanceys called it. Over the four nights of ball, the teams would attempt to work toward and achieve a tie that lasted through three overtimes.

So the play, with the ball, bounced back and forth. The Omegans' starting team proved to be runners and gunners. They were initially hot-handed and managed at one point a fifteen-point lead over the Alphaites. But then the Omegans tired and shuffled in reserves, and over the next thirty minutes the Alphaites fought back from their deficit and maintained a steady four- to eight-point lead. The first night's competition ended with the Alphaites leading by six.

And it was a true competition. No players played under their abilities or in any way attempted to throw a game. On the second night, the Omegan coach started a mixture of two gunners with three teenaged, disciplined players, then alternated in her other sharpshooters as the night progressed. The second game ended with a thrilling long shot, practically from half court, that broke a tie and put the Omegans on top by three points. Steadily the coaches and teams were learning what combination of players, pitted most strategically against the other team's particular players and their strengths and weaknesses, would inch them closer to two magnificently matched squads.

Technically, if a three-overtime tie was achieved, the Great Game could end on the third night. But on that evening the Omegans managed to break out of the second overtime with a four-point lead. So the game went into its fourth night. The gymnasium was packed. The Alphaites had perfected a half-court zone defense that nullified the Omegans' superior abilities as shooters and slowed the pace of the game. Somehow, late into the night, the teams had accomplished two overtimes. The crowd thundered with excitement as the third overtime began. There were years, after all, when the three-overtime tie was not achieved, and on those years the Great Game would be considered something of a failure. Everyone now bent their wills toward the tie that binds.

As the third overtime ticked into its final thirty seconds, the Omegans held a three-point lead. The Alphaites advanced the ball downcourt. A spindly teenager, not the best ball handler, almost had the ball stolen by a fresh Omegan substitute. The ball bobbled back and forth between the competing players. The crowd held its breath. The teen had a height advantage, if not an advantage in coordination, and at last swatted the ball away from his pestering opponent. It flew over the heads of two Omegan forwards and into the hands of an Alphaite guard. Ten seconds on the clock.

Nine . . . Eight . . . Omegans swarmed the Alphaite and had him all but trapped. Then he bounce-passed the ball into the hands of the seventyish woman, the oldest player on his team. She was behind the three-point line, but unbothered by Omegan defenders since they doubted the adequacy of her strength to hit the long-distance shot. The crowd began chanting: "Six! Five! Four!" The dear woman squared up. She had played in the Great Game for decades, but this could be her highest moment of glory. Or her moment of deepest humiliation. "Two! One!" the crowd roared. She sent the ball flying. She put a strong but light touch on it. It arched beautifully into the backboard, then to the front lip of the hoop. The buzzer squawked. The ball bounced to the back of the hoop, then back again to the front. With the buzzer still sounding, it dropped into the net.

All the players, from both teams, rushed the court, congratulating the old woman. Onlookers flooded out of the stands and onto the floor. The tying shooter was lifted onto shoulders and paraded through the gleeful crowds, all but losing her eyeglasses as she was jostled from one set of shoulders to another. Tears streamed down her cheeks and she lifted her fists high in triumph and elation. Donald and Joy were screaming themselves hoarse. And Al realized he was on his feet, pounding his hands together, shouting as loudly as he could manage.

For years after in the Comp Cities, they would say this was the greatest of the Great Games.

❧

Reba Wilding was back in town the next day. She said she would never forgive herself for missing the Great Game, and this one most especially. But what can you do? Church business had taken precedence; a Catholic was someone who could respond to authority even at real sacrifice.

Although the game had lasted past midnight, and celebrations extended longer, Al insisted that Joy escort him to the church and introduce him to Wilding as soon as she was expected in the church office, at 9 a.m. Extending her wonderful hospitality to the end, Joy agreed.

Greeting Reba, Al offered up the Romans 16 code word. Reba answered in kind. She sensed Al's overweening eagerness for news on Valerie, so she only teased him for a minute or two, then cut to the chase. Valerie had been escorted from the Comp Cities to a town in southwestern Kansas, a town named Old Liberal. It was only a couple of hundred miles from the Comp Cities.

Al could not believe his ears. He asked Reba to repeat herself. And when she did, happily, Al knew that the last leg of his journey would begin immediately, that very afternoon.

20

Al had to forcibly pace himself. He was so close to Valerie; the end of his journey was in sight. He proceeded through the Flint Hills and on south like a man afire.

But after a few days of journeying, he sensed anxiety as well as anticipation growing. The familiar worries returned. What if Valerie had made it to her place of refuge, and since died? He could not believe she was dead, after all he had suffered, after all she had surely suffered and undergone on her trip to safety.

There were other worries and possibilities, though, and these loomed large and seemed all too credible. Five long years had passed. How did he know that in that interim Valerie had not met another man, had not taken a husband? The familiar tinges of melancholia, which the busyness and excitement and trials of his journey had eclipsed, now returned to consciousness.

He imagined how easily, how many, men would desire her as a companion. He found himself praying that she remained single and unattached. Then he realized that this hope and prayer, taken to its conclusion, entailed that he would rather wish her dead than committed to another man. Was that what he wanted? No, by no means, no! So he recognized, not eagerly, that he must begin to pray not just that she was alive and awaited *him,* but simply for her own welfare: that she was alive and well, whether or not she awaited him.

Al was struck by the wisdom of the Christian tradition. The tradition saw sin, at its root, as an attempt of the creature to become a god, to rule over the world and its sometimes unwelcome contingencies against one's own benefit and ease. But the creature, a single mortal, while wonderful in itself, was made puny and mean by grasping at godhood. Al was not and never would or should be Valerie's god, the source of all her life and sustenance, without which she would cease to be.

So he began to pray for her welfare and goodness, for her attachment to the one true God—the only reality big enough and compassionate enough to sustain creation and all its creatures. And Al prayed for Val's welfare and good apart from Al's own wishes and desires. "Keep her, God," he prayed. "Keep her well for her sake and for your sake. This first and foremost, and finally, whatever it entails for me."

He learned the prayer and knew himself a better man for being able to pray it. At the same time, he recognized with new appreciation the Lord's Prayer's petition that God would lead us not into temptation or testing. So he just as earnestly prayed that he would not be tested by the loss of Valerie. And he added to his prayer for Valerie the "if it be your will" codicil: "I pray for her good apart from my own, gracious God. But still, if it be your will, let her be there for me. For the two of us."

❧

After ten days of travel, Al estimated himself only ten or twenty miles from his final destination of Old Liberal. The sun was setting and the evening light threw shadows long and aslant. He knew he would reluctantly have to stop and set up camp for the night. He came adjacent to a copse of trees, a sweet spot for gathering firewood and preparing some dinner.

He had gathered a couple of handfuls of kindling when he noticed birdsong in the surrounding trees ceasing. Then he took in a sharp smell, a stink of the road and cheap tobacco and drink sour with vomit. He turned around to find three men facing him. A bare-armed man with enormous eyebrows that twitched wildly, like spastic caterpillars, was the apparent leader. He spoke: "Hello, stranger. How's about you just give us your food and money, and we'll move on."

Later Al would reflect that he might have talked with the men, tried to negotiate, and if necessary simply have given them his possessions. After all, he was nearly at Old Liberal, where he would hopefully find Valerie and where, at any event, he could work and earn money and supplies for his return to Old Chicago. But in the moment, Al reacted instinctively. He leapt on a fallen log that lay between him and the men. One man lunged forward at him, and Al jerked a knee up under his chin. There was a sickening thud. Now the men were enraged. A second man swung and hit Al, hard, in the stomach. All the breath rushed from Al's lungs and he crashed off the log. The eyebrowed man laughed sourly. The man who knocked Al off the log kicked him repeatedly in the ribs and abdomen. Al heard, as from a muffled distance, a sharp crack in his chest area. The eyebrowed man stepped forward and stomped at Al's crotch, landing at least two enormously painful blows.

Then the man Al had caught under the jaw recovered his feet and found a club of wood. "Let me at the bastard," he cried. He swung so wildly the other two men stepped aside. He struck Al several times in the torso and moved his strikes upward. Two times, with wide swings, he hit Al in the head. Al felt warm blood flowing down his face and from his mouth before he lost consciousness. The leader of the band pushed the clubbing man back and looked down on the crumpled, bloodied form at their feet. The three men went silent for a moment.

"Looks like we've killed him," the leader said. He swatted the clubber in the shoulder and cursed. "We'll have to bury the son of a bitch. He's too close to the road. Start diggin'."

The eyebrowed man rifled Al's pockets and, in doing so, found his money belt. "Ah ha," he said with a grim smile. They dragged Al away from the trees and their roots. Then they dug with their hands and sticks. They swore and sweated, and eventually they had achieved a crude hole, about four feet deep, and not too long. They shoved Al's limp body in the hole and he landed on crumpled knees. The clubber used his boot to compress Al farther into the hole, and gave one last stamp on his head. They covered the hole and the clubber finally stood atop the protruding pile and stomped the sandy dirt firm.

The men looked around and confirmed that they remained unobserved. The birds had resumed their singing as the three men hastily departed the sloppy grave.

21

Coyote watched from a ridge just above the copse of trees. He was a scavenger, with centuries of scavenging in his bones. His ancestors had scavenged these plains for uncountable risings and settings of the fireball in the sky. They scavenged dead and dying jackrabbits, hawks, prairie dogs, the mutilated carcasses of deer and buffalo. Often they subsisted on little more than the paper-thin remains of sparrows and dried snakes. They would roam for days without any kind of meal. Oftentimes they would succumb themselves, and become meat for their starving fellows. They scavenged before any people were here, and they had scavenged as the first people appeared and hunted the buffalo. They continued to scavenge over the decades more, during which people appeared and hunted both the buffalo and the people who had first hunted the buffalo.

Coyote was one of the scavengers' kind. He was a ragged suit of mangy, scabby hair on bones. He was almost always hungry, and hunger kept him on the move. He lived by his wits, such as they were. By his wits, and by great caution.

He was investigating the ridge earlier in the day when he saw the first man appear. He lay down and still, watching and waiting. Often men would leave behind scraps, little bites to quiet his growling belly for a while. He was still waiting when the other men appeared. Then the men fought. Coyote did not care that they fought or why they fought. Though he could guess they fought over food, it was always a mystery to him that men so often fought even when there was plenty of food at hand for them, and would even leave meat behind after their seemingly endless bouts of violence.

Not long after the men attacked the other man, Coyote smelled the tangy iron of blood in the air. He salivated and shifted restlessly, but only slightly. He must make himself wait. He would see what would unfold.

He could hardly believe it when the men dragged the broken man and dumped him in a hole. So much meat! And again the men were wasting it. Coyote's last meal was a distant memory, a bit of stiff meat and hide he gnawed off a maggoty cow that had already been picked over. Fresh meat was a rarity, and here was an undreamable abundance of it. He drew deep drafts of air into his nostrils to determine if other beasts were in the area, and detected none. Quiet as the mildest breeze, he turned and looked behind himself and in all directions. The plains were as empty as the great sky that arched over them. Coyote felt overpowering eagerness, his hunger sharpened. But he held himself still.

Eventually the attackers moved away. Their odor was rank—sour and bitter and strong. But the sweet waft of fresh blood remained robust in his nostrils, or at least in his memory. He had to concentrate on the attackers' smells, making sure they had really disappeared from the scene. And still, before moving, he tested again the wind in all directions.

He sniffed and listened, then he looked all about. He took two steps forward and stopped. Sniffed, listened, looked. He took more steps, then froze again. There were new smells in the air. He registered them as small animal smells emanating from the copse. It was safe to go ahead. He trotted a few steps and stopped. Once again: sniff, listen, look. And so forth.

At last he was at the aborted campsite. Here the sour and bitter smells of the attackers lingered. He stopped until he was certain they were only trace odors. He examined scuffle marks in the dirt, nosed at a broken twig or two. He stood above the grave. One last time he tested the air, listened, and looked all around himself. Then, finally freeing himself and no longer resisting his hunger, he pawed at the top of the hole. He scratched vigorously, threw dirt between his back legs. A man's hand appeared, wet with blood and soaked dirt. Ravenously, coyote licked the back of the hand, then pushed it over at the wrist and licked the palm clean too. Saliva ran freely between his teeth. He dug all the more furiously.

Now the man's slumped head appeared. Coyote propped his snout under the man's jaw and pushed the head back. He was in the act of lunging at the throat when, suddenly, the man groaned, took in a great, gagging breath, and coughed a gout of blood from his mouth.

Coyote's instincts for immediate survival rushed and overtook his instincts of hunger. Coyote fled, never looking back. But before he was gone, Al opened his eyes and beheld his liberator, a scroungy beast now beating its way across the prairie.

22

Freed by the coyote, Al shifted dirt from himself and then gingerly and wobbly stood up in the grave. Soil streamed down his body in a small avalanche and settled around his feet. With effort, Al pulled his boots from the pit. Then he collapsed on the ground beside the grave. He crawled a few feet. He pushed himself up on his knees, swayed dizzily. Then he uneasily stood again. His head throbbed and ached. He tongued at some loose teeth. Sharp pains shot across his chest—he figured he had some broken ribs. Blood was caking across his forehead and eyes and chin. His shirt was stiff and sticky from the same blood. He staggered once around the campsite, ascertaining that he could walk. He was alive, after all. And his mission—to join Val now that he was so close to her—flooded back into consciousness. But at the moment he was too sore and hurt to move on. He wanted, immediately, nothing other than rest. He found his torn jacket, lay down, and pulled it over himself as a makeshift blanket. Then he collapsed into a deep, reeling sleep.

He awoke to the bray of a mule.

"Hush, Henry," said a tall, willowy woman who sat beside a crackling fire. She spoke in a whispery rasp, as if with a sandpaper larynx.

"Morning, stranger," the woman said. "I hope you don't mind that I used your firewood to start us a breakfast."

Al sat up. He looked a sight, slimed with dirt and blood, mud pasted in his hair.

"You look a little worse for the wear," the woman commented.

"And I don't feel too great," Al said. "Some thugs attacked me. And with my own firewood," he added, somehow managing a joke. "I'm glad to have that wood put to a more pleasing use."

The woman laughed softly. She introduced herself as Gail. She saw Al wince and press at his chest. "They probably cracked a rib or two," she said. "Here."

Gail went to the mule-hitched wagon and dug around its flat wooden bed. With grunts and a clatter of junk, she extricated some rags, ripped them into the strips, and tied three around Al's chest.

Gail had beans and coffee boiling. She handed Al a steaming cup of the coffee and a piece of sourdough bread. He ate the bread hungrily. And when she ladled out a bowl of beans, he ate them eagerly too.

"Where you headed?" Gail asked after they finished breakfast.

"To Old Liberal."

"I'm headed that way. You just as well ride with me." Gail gathered her pots and pans into a burlap bag. She dropped it in the wagon. She busted a bail of hay and spread some straw on the wagon bed. "This'll give you a little softer ride," she said, and helped Al aboard.

Directly she clicked her tongue, muttered, "Get along, Henry," and the wagon creaked down the road. Gail kept the mule at a walk, but still Al bounced in the bed. Every bounce hurt. Al quickly determined that getting flat on his back was the most comfortable position he could achieve. He watched the blue sky and puffy white clouds roll overhead, hawks gliding and spiraling on thermals. He listened to birdsong, to Gail humming contentedly, and dozed.

❧

But Al didn't doze for long. Within hours he would at last reach Old Liberal and Valerie. Despite his aches and pains, excitement surged and lifted Al's spirits. He mused to himself a prayer of thanksgiving, that he had survived the beating and made it this far.

Yet it seemed odd to think that God would let him be hurt. Al really was thankful, but if prayers were effective, why didn't God protect him from getting beaten and buried in the first place? Al thought that on the one hand prayers were about aligning ourselves with God and the way the world really is, created and sustained by God the Father. So part of what prayers did was change us, the pray-ers. Yet we prayed for more than just change in our personal, psychological, and spiritual states or conditions. We prayed for safe travel, for success in godly endeavors, for good crops, for physical healing, for the welfare of loved ones in danger.

So our prayers indicated belief and hope that God would intervene, that God would act and make a difference in the world, and not just in our thoughts and feelings. The ultimate hope, of course, was that God was at work redeeming all of creation, bringing his kingdom to its fullness and consummation "on earth as in heaven," in the words of the Lord's Prayer. "God so loved the *world*," said the famous verse in the Gospel of John. The Apostle Paul was clear that he expected God to renew the heavens and the earth, that our bodies would be raised to inhabit that new creation. The Old Testament prophets and the book of Revelation expected a new world, too.

That was a long work, Al mused, the work of making a new world out of this tired, tattered, old world. It was a work that spanned centuries. God worked for thousands of years in and through the people Israel, then through Christ and the church. Despite the moral and imaginative failings of his people—the reservations of Moses, the missteps of King David, the obduracy and dimness of the apostles—God had kept working to bring his kingdom into the world. Often plans A and B had failed, and yet God had stayed at it, stayed at it through plan C, all the way down to plans X, Y, and Z-plus if he had to. God worked with his people through the vagaries of their slavery and failed monarchy and exile.

So God was able to "fall back" on contingency plans, ever able to invent and reinvent toward his ends and goals for humanity and creation. Any individual, Al included, was a small, small part in this overarching story, serving toward the healing of creation a tiny step at a time. And if God could work through setbacks in the larger, ultimate plan, why could God not do the same in the lives of individuals? God might not—God clearly did not—work to prevent all the ills that might befall his creatures. But so long as a creature, a man or a woman or a child, remained with a key and important role to play, God would preserve him or her for that part. He would preserve his servant until that part was finished, and in the event of how ever many setbacks, miscues, and perils occurred along the way. If God could send the faltering servant Balaam an ass, a donkey who spoke truth, God could send his servant Albert a coyote. A hungry, scrounging coyote that unwittingly saved Al's life. And so God had. And so God worked not only through tragedy, but through comedy.

Such were Al's thoughts as he jounced along in the wagon. His excitement was barely containable, but he felt a sense of peace beneath the vast prairie sky.

Excited as he was, Al tried to contain himself as Gail's wagon creaked and swayed into the outskirts of Old Liberal. It might be hours, even a day or so, before he located Val in this sizeable town. The wagon rolled past shops, past a scattering of people on the sidewalks, past barking dogs that nipped at its wheels. Soon there were more and louder voices, clusters of people gathered around a spring. Children splashed in the spring's shallows. Women and men scrubbed at dirty laundry. A few stood up to their ankles in water, smoking and talking. Al casually scanned faces, some smiling, some squinting in the blinding white sunlight.

The first he saw—and realized—of her was her hair and shoulders. Valerie's hair and shoulders. She had turned to look at the passing wagon, was wringing water from a shirt. She wore jean shorts and a red tank top. She was beautiful beyond any of his memories. And there she was, on the other side of the spring.

Al scurried off the wagon while it remained in motion. He reeled forward a few feet and lost his footing, dropped into the sand around the spring. He was trying to speak but was most intent on moving forward, toward her, to her. He hobbled headlong into the pool. He fell again. He tasted the iron in the water and felt it violently shoot up his nostrils. But he kept moving forward, half walking, half swimming. Then he was back upright, slogging, striding, water flying around him and glinting in the glaring light.

An onlooker or two squealed. They gave him a wide berth—this strange man, bloodied and bruised, flailing through the water, grunting and churning.

Back up, Albert saw, registered it for the first time, that Valerie was not alone. There was a small boy of five or six years beside her. The boy looked startled and scared at the strange man crashing through the water toward him.

At first Valerie looked startled too. Then her eyes went from blank to a piercing focus, and tears abruptly burst from them. She cried out, a moan that transformed into a shout, a shout of surprised and unbelieving joy.

And Albert roared forward, parting the water, willing it aside, daring it to take him down again, when no ocean could. He neared Valerie. He made one last surge and wrapped her in his arms.

"You came, you came," she whispered into his ear.

And he sputtered through water and tears, finally possessing a voice: "Valerie! Valerie! Valerie!" Then followed the question he had to ask: "Are you married?"

"Only married in spirit to you," she said with a brilliant smile. "One of the first things we need to do is make it official. After all, we've already started a family."

Dried and rewetted blood and mud streaked down his face and arms. He thought somewhere, far back in his mind, but clear as the midday sun, that this was a baptism, his second baptism. He had come through fire, through lunatic armies and religious fanatics and ghostly Indians and stampeding buffalo and a time in his own grave, and now at last he had arrived, and the baptism climaxed and was completed in water. What it meant was that he was a new man. Behind him was the death of loneliness, the grinding death of his separation from Val. Before him was new life with her.

And, apparently, with this boy. Val and Al hugged and kissed, broke and then rehugged, squeezing one another desperately. After some moments, Val gestured toward the towheaded boy and said, "I need to introduce you. To your son."

Still holding Val with one arm, Al pivoted and looked down at the boy.

"His name is Albert Junior," Val said.

And then Al saw that the boy's eyes were familiar. They shone gray and rested in slanted pockets. They were kind and lively and behind them was toughness and courage. Albert Junior's eyes were the eyes of his grandfather, Ray Simmel. Al looked at his son and he saw his father. Now Al had not only a second baptism but a second chance. Al reached out and grasped the boy's hand. He gripped the hand and knew that he would never, ever let this grip falter, this grasp break, this instant and undying love subside.

Acknowledgments

B. J. Heyboer was the first reader of this novel, in an early draft. She had helpful criticisms and suggestions. Most importantly, she encouraged me to keep at it and bring it to fruition. She is a gifted encourager, and I would not have finished the book without her cheerleading.

I am thankful to Charlie Collier, Jacob Martin, and the other editors and staff at Cascade. Charlie is a joy to work with, and I appreciate his willingness to take on my first novel. The gang at Wipf and Stock is at once unfailingly able and delightfully eccentric. Thanks to Jon Stock and John Wipf for starting and sustaining the whole crazy and wonderful enterprise.

Some supporting books behind this book should be mentioned. In the chapters about Girardsville, theologically informed readers will recognize the work of René Girard lurking in the background. I drew especially on his *I See Satan Fall Like Lightning* (Orbis, 2001) and *The Girard Reader* (Crossroad, 2001). I learned much about the habits and environs of buffalo (technically, bison) from Dale F. Lott, *American Bison: A Natural History* (University of California Press, 2003) and first heard of the restored Buffalo Commons in conversation with Dwight Baker. The chapters on the meta-Indians, with their depiction of a ghost dance, owe a great deal to Michael Hittman, *Wovoka and the Ghost Dance* (University of Nebraska Press, 1990) and Alice Beck Kehoe, *The Ghost Dance: Ethnohistory and Revitalization* (Waveland, 2006).

One of the great joys of my life is that my daughter, Jesselyn Ewing, now works with me at Cascade. More computer savvy than I, Jess helped me with formatting and other issues in the late stages of this book. She hasn't gotten around to reading the book yet, but then I keep shoveling other books her way to edit—which she does ever so capably.

I could have never written the book without the encouragement and vital help of my wife, Sandy. In this case I owe much to her willingness to take on more than her share of housework as I spent Saturdays at the writing desk. Sandy is a lifegiver of the highest magnitude, and I am a primary recipient of her gifts and sustaining ways. I hope you like this one, honey.

www.ingramcontent.com/pod-product-compliance
Lightning Source LLC
Chambersburg PA
CBHW020743020826
48980CB00019B/771/J
* 9 7 8 1 4 9 8 2 8 5 3 2 2 *